Yukon Secret Agents

Yukon Secret Agents

A Boy's Adventure during the Alaska Border Dispute

MacBride Museum Yukon Kids Series

Keith Halliday

Illustrations by Kieran, Aline and Pascale Halliday

iUniverse, Inc.

New York Lincoln Shanghai

Yukon Secret Agents
A Boy's Adventure during the Alaska Border Dispute

Copyright © 2007 by Keith Halliday

iUniverse books may be ordered through booksellers or by contacting:

iUniverse
2021 Pine Lake Road, Suite 100
Lincoln, NE 68512
www.iuniverse.com
1-800-Authors (1-800-288-4677)

This is a work of fiction. All of the characters, names, incidents, organizations, and dialogue in this novel are either the products of the author's imagination or are used fictitiously.

All images and photos are © 2007 by Keith Halliday, except for images generously provided by the MacBride Museum or as noted otherwise.

ISBN: 978-0-595-44272-0 (pbk)
ISBN: 978-0-595-88602-9 (ebk)

Printed in the United States of America

To my son Kieran and my
grandfather Bill Taylor, both Yukon boys

Contents

Foreword

This astonishing and apparently true adventure during the Alaska-Canada boundary dispute was written over 100 years ago by a twelve-year-old Yukon boy named Kip Dutoit, who had startling first hand access to U.S. President Theodore Roosevelt and North West Mounted Police hero Sam Steele. The document was recently discovered in a forgotten safe deposit box in a musty envelope marked "Do Not Open Before 2003." It comes less than a year after the equally remarkable discovery of the 1898 Gold Rush diary of Kip's step-sister, Aurore.

The Kip Dutoit papers provide a fresh new view of the Alaska-Canada border dispute of 1903, a major international incident that almost led to war between the United States, Britain and Canada. As Kip reminds us, this was when President Roosevelt said "Walk softly but carry a big stick," and sent hundreds of U.S. Army soldiers to Alaska to make his point.

Kip's story takes us on an exciting ride from the Yukon River to the Chilkoot Pass, from the mining explosion that almost killed his father to a wild train chase, and from the exploits of famous Klondike lawman Sam Steele to the fiendish plots of Black Moran. Throughout it all, as Kip points out himself, we glimpse the North's renowned pioneer spirit: courage, selfless sacrifice and rugged self-reliance.

Finding the Kip Dutoit papers raised many questions. Why did he write the story and not publish it? Why were the papers found with a strangely vague letter addressed to Kip from the British Foreign Office in London? And then there was the remarkable note from

President Roosevelt himself: "Ripping story, Kip! Without you there would've been a dust up that would have made the War of 1812 look like Sunday School bickering!"

Then archivists at the Canadian Department of Foreign Affairs noticed some apparently meaningless letters on the top of the first sheet: "45001/Y01/013." Experts in diplomatic history—or readers of Rudyard Kipling—will immediately see the connection. British Intelligence used such numbers to identify its agents in the early 20th Century.

In fact, it has emerged that 45001 was the British Secret Service's code number for Major Percy Brown. Percy is famous as the "Piccadilly Dude" in Robert Service's poem "The Ballad of the Ice Worm Cocktail." In real life, he was also with British Intelligence in Washington in 1903. Y01 would have been one of his agents. And this was report number 13.

Could Kip really have been agent Y01? Report 13 is listed in the declassified archives in London, but the report itself is missing. Interestingly, it was checked out by Percy in 1904 and never returned. When you read the story, we think you'll guess why.

Kip seems to have shared the story with the U.S. government too, or at least with the president. Remarkably, Kip earned the gratitude of both sides of the dispute!

The story also includes some remarkable new information about President Roosevelt. The role of Kip and Aurore in convincing the president to establish Yosemite Park and the U.S. National Parks Service is remarkable. It is well known that the "Teddy Bear" is named after Theodore Roosevelt, but until now we didn't know how he came up with the idea.

We have done a minimum of editing to Kip's story. We have corrected some spelling errors and have updated the place names: Whitehorse instead of White Horse, for example. For readers who want to learn more about the 1903 Alaska-Canada boundary dispute, we have also included Kip's 1903 school essay on the topic in the appendix of this book. You'll see why Kip's teacher, Mr. Galpin, gave him an "A+." We also include some of Kip's drawings. Finally, we have added a few historical notes of our own. They appear as footnotes in the version you are about to read.

Kip never spoke publicly about his adventures. Nor did his siblings Aurore, Papillon and Yves. But we know the four of them talked about it as Kip lay dying in his hospital room eighty years later. Kip's shaky handwriting is still visible on the cover: "Aurore, take this to the safe deposit box and mark it '2003'. I promised Sam Steele I'd never tell, but I figure 100 years is close enough."

We think you will enjoy the tale, as President Roosevelt did, and understand why Kip remembered it to his last day.

Professor H. I. Story
Whitehorse, Yukon Territory
2007

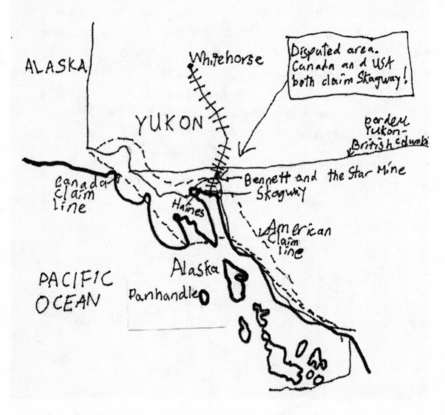

the Alaska Boundary Dispute 1903
By Kip Dutoit

ALASKA

Whitehorse

Disputed area.
Canada and USA
both claim Skagway!

YUKON

border
Yukon–
British columbia

Canada
claim
line

Bennett and the Star Mine

Skagway

Haines

American
claim
line

PACIFIC
OCEAN

Alaska
Panhandle

Above: A map discovered with Kip's papers, showing how both Canada and the United States claimed the ports of Skagway and Haines. Bennett, the Star Mine and the White Pass and Yukon Route railway are also shown.

Chapter 1

Explosion on Lake Bennett

45001/Y01/013

I will never forget my Dad's last words before the explosion. He was mad. "Kip! Be more careful with those boxes! You don't know what's in them!"

We were unloading Dad's boat at the Star Mine on Lake Bennett and I had just tried to carry two boxes at once. They were too heavy and I dropped one on the dock.

Dad had told me the same thing three times already that day. He reminded me of that too. But this time he grabbed me by the shoulder. His eyes sparkled fiercely and he looked right at me. He didn't need to say anything else. I knew what he was thinking. "You're a smart kid ... why don't you listen?" Or "Haste makes waste." Or "That's the third time I've said 'careful!'"

"All right! I get it!" I said angrily. I was mad too. Why was he always pushing me to be perfect? I twisted my shoulder out of his grip and stomped back to the boat for another load.

Rudi von Neidling smirked at me. He was standing on top of a crate of baked beans with the steep, rocky slopes of the mountain right behind him. His father owned the Star Mine. "You got trouble understanding English?" he laughed. He loved making fun of my brother Yves and me as "frogs" because we spoke French at home.

It really bugged me, especially since whenever I reminded him that he and his father spoke German, he would tell the teacher I was teasing him and I'd get in trouble.

Anyway, that's when the explosion happened. I didn't hear it. I don't know why.

But I felt it.

One second I was bending down to pick up another box marked "Star Mine." The next I was on my back like I'd been given the worst body check in the history of hockey. At first, I didn't know what had happened. I sat up. Believe it or not, I scratched my head.

There was still no sound. At least that's how I remember it. I looked around in a daze, trying to figure out what had happened. A puff of smoke was going straight up from the Star Mine's dock. "I wonder what that is?" I asked myself dreamily.

Then I heard a scream and a rock the size of a pumpkin landed beside me. It hit a case of canned milk like a cannon ball and sprayed me with sweet, sticky goo.

"Run for it!" shouted my Dad. "The rocks'll kill you!" That got me going. I jumped up in a second. I saw our dog D'Artagnan leap off the dock into the water and start swimming furiously. I ran for our boat.

A case of beans came down from the sky like a meteor and landed in Lake Bennett beside the boat. A huge fountain of water drenched me.

Just at that moment my little brother Yves stuck his head up the stairs to look around. He always seems to know when something interesting is going on. I could see him looking at a tin of milk that was still bouncing around the deck.

"En bas!" I shouted in French. "Get below!"

"Get lost, big brother!" he shouted back with his usual smile. He thought I was bossing him around. There was no time to argue. I just put my foot on his chest and pushed him down the stairs. Then I jumped down after him.

We sat under the deck as rocks and canned goods pelted the boat. It was like being in an old cabin in a thunderstorm, except that the raindrops weighed ten pounds. We crawled under a bench for more protection and huddled in the dark.

It was scary. I could feel Yves hugging me like he did when he was little and had a nightmare. I tried to sing him "Frère Jacques" like I used to but I didn't even get to "Dormez-vous?"

Then there was a huge smash and the whole boat shuddered. Suddenly it wasn't dark any more. It wasn't dry either. Something huge had just crashed through our boat's deck and gone right out through the bottom. Water gushed in.

"Get out!" I shouted. Yves didn't have to be told twice. He was up the ladder in one leap and over the side into Lake Bennett. I was right after him.

We dived deep to try to avoid the rocks. I don't know if this would have helped us, but by the time we came up for air the rocks had stopped falling.

Now I could hear noises. Everyone seemed to be screaming at once. Gurgling noises and steam came out of our boat as it slowly sank beside the dock. Scraps of paper, firewood and a box of eggs bobbed in the water. Little drops of oil bobbed up to the surface then spread out, making little rainbows on the water. More importantly, I suddenly noticed that Lake Bennett is freezing cold, even in June.

I looked around for Yves. He had his arms around D'Artagnan's neck and was swimming back to shore. We scrambled out of the water. "Let's find Dad and tell him we're all right," I told Yves. I held my hand up to shade my eyes from the Yukon sun as I scanned the dock. There was no sign of him. Yves was calling his name.

I felt Yves reach for my hand. "Kip, I'm scared," he said. He's just little, but he has this strange sense for things.

Then we saw my Dad. His legs were sticking out from behind a pile of boxes. His left foot was pointed a funny direction.

He wasn't moving.

We ran over. His head was covered in blood. Not just a little. It was pouring out onto the dock and spreading like spilled ink at school.

Except it was bright, bright red.

I've had bad things happen to me before. I've broken my arm. The chimney caught fire and almost burned our cabin down in the middle of winter. My stepmother got the fever and was so sick that the priest came and we stayed up all night in case she died.

But nothing prepares you to see your Dad lying perfectly still in a pool of blood.

I ran over and knelt beside him. A few other men ran over too. Everybody knew my Dad.

"Oh Lord!" said one of the men.

"Don't talk like that! Especially in front of his sons!" snapped another. It was Mr. Liebherr. I knew him from Whitehorse. He didn't smile much and was pretty gruff, but he was decent. He was German and had a strong accent. Sometimes, I could barely understand him.

Yves and I just stood there. We didn't know what to do. Mr. Liebherr took off his shirt and pressed it against my Dad's head where the bleeding was the worst.

Suddenly, the shadow of another man appeared. "What happened here?" he shouted angrily. All I could see in the sun was a black shape. It was Rudi's father, Captain von Neidling.

No one said anything. Except Rudi. He pointed at me.

"That boy was throwing boxes around. Then the explosion happened."

Everybody turned to me. I looked down at my Dad. My voice didn't seem to work.

Rudi's Dad said something in German. A swear word. Then he said, "Idiot! Be careful with the explosives or you'll all end up dead!" Then he started shouting at the other men. "Get back to work or I'll dock your pay. Clean this up! Fix that pipe! Get those boxes into the shed before it rains!" He was shouting orders to all of the men. Everybody jumped up and started running around.

Except Mr. Liebherr, that is. He was still crouching over my Dad. I don't think he heard anything Captain von Neidling had said.

"Liebherr!" shouted Rudi's father again. His German accent was strong. Now that I could see him, he was tall and still looked athletic. There was a little bit of grey hair beginning to show on his temples. His face was cleanly shaven. But the thing you noticed first was his old captain's hat from the German Navy, which he wore all the time. At school Rudi said he was an admiral, but Mr. Liebherr told me later he was just a captain.

The second thing you noticed was how Captain von Neidling looked at you. Mr. Liebherr called it "intensity."

Right behind him was Black Moran.[1] Captain von Neidling called Black Moran a "business associate," but Black Moran didn't look like any regular Yukon businessman to me. I don't think businessmen are supposed to carry guns or have nicknames like "Black."

They say Black Moran was a member of Soapy Smith's gang, but no one knows for sure.

Believe it or not, he says quotes from the Bible all the time and we used to see him every Sunday at church. Once we had a visiting priest from Alaska and he got so nervous when he saw Black Moran in line for communion that he dropped the cup!

Anyway, Black Moran stared at us from under his battered black Stetson hat, rubbing his black whiskers like seeing Dad bleeding was the most boring thing he ever saw. He pulled a cigarette out of his pocket.

---

1.   Editor's note: this is the first historical evidence that Black Moran really existed. He is described in several Robert Service poems as the fastest gun in Alaska. He faced down crooked Sheriff Red McGraw in "The Duel." In "Black Moran," he robs a sleigh carrying two gamblers. When he discovers the third passenger is a priest, he donates his loot to the Church after making the gamblers pray at gunpoint.

"It rained fire and brimstone from heaven, and destroyed them all. Luke 17:29," said Black Moran in a quiet, raspy voice. Then he sparked a match and lit his cigarette.

But Captain von Neidling wasn't paying attention to Black Moran. He was staring intensely at Mr. Liebherr. "Liebherr!" he shouted. "What are you doing! Time is money! Let that fellow care for himself and get these others back to work."

Suddenly, I got very angry. Neidling and Black Moran didn't care about my Dad at all. "That's my Dad!" I shouted. "He's hurt!"

"And his boat has sunk carrying *my* cargo," said Captain von Neidling coldly.

Mr. Liebherr stood up and looked Captain von Neidling in the eye. "I'll be taking the row boat across to Bennett to get this gentleman to Dr. Nicholson in Whitehorse." His voice was tough. He wasn't asking for permission.

Captain von Neidling rolled his eyes. "If you insist," he said to Mr. Liebherr. To Black Moran he said, "Stop Liebherr's pay until he gets back."

Mr. Liebherr and some of the other men carried Dad to the row-boat. I took off my jacket and put it as a pillow under my Dad's head. Yves and D'Artagnan jumped in, Mr. Liebherr cast off the stern rope and I did the same in the bow.

Rudi waited until his father's back was turned. Then he picked up a rock and threw it at us. "Frogs!" he yelled with a laugh as the rock splashed beside the boat.

"Don't you mind that, Kip," said Mr. Liebherr kindly. "Captain von Neidling wasn't very popular in Africa either. Now just keep an eye over my shoulder and keep me on course as I row us across the lake to the train." As we rowed, Mr. Liebherr kept us distracted by telling us about the German colonies in Southwest Africa, where he used to live before he heard about the Klondike Gold Rush and went to the Yukon. As we reached shore, he laughed. It was a bitter kind of laugh. "Neidling's African mine didn't have any gold either. He should have stayed in the navy!"

We loaded Dad onto the train. The conductor stretched out a sleeping bag on the floor for him. The conductor wanted tickets. We didn't have any, but Mr. Liebherr pulled out his wallet and bought us some. "And a ticket for me too," he said. "Stopping my pay for taking a man to the doctor? I worked for him once in Africa. And once here. That's it!"

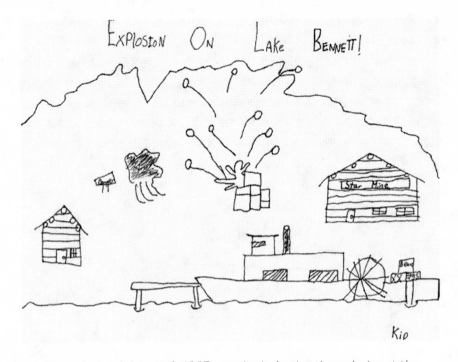

Above: A sketch from Kip's 1903 scrapbook showing the explosion at the Star Mine, the dock and the family's boat where Kip and Yves hid from falling rocks.

Chapter 2

Dr. Nicholson's Kitchen Table

The train back to Whitehorse seemed to take forever. It was really only five hours. But that's a long time when you are trying to get your Dad to the doctor.

Yves was very upset. I was scared too. But I knew I had to help Yves. So I told him some hockey stories. His favourite story is how the Montreal AAAs beat Winnipeg two games to one in the Stanley Cup last year. We're both big Montreal fans of course. He loves the part about how they had to replay Game 2 since they went into over-time but had to stop because of the city curfew![1]

My story worked. Yves was soon thinking only about hockey. "The Yukon should challenge for the Stanley Cup!" he said enthusiastically.

"Yeah! I should tell Mr. Boyle! I bet he could talk Weldy Young into playing. It would sure be great to see a real game like that instead

---

1.   Editor's Note: Kip is right. The 1903 Stanley Cup series between the Montreal Amateur Athletic Association and the Winnipeg Victorias is the only series in Stanley Cup history where a game had to be replayed. Winnipeg won the replayed second game, but lost 4-1 to Montreal in the decisive third game. At the time, before the National Hockey League, the champion of any hockey league could challenge the Stanley Cup holder. The Montreal AAA and the Montreal Wanderers were the dominant Montreal teams at the time. The Montreal Canadiens weren't started until several years later.

of having to read about it two weeks later in Mr. Taylor's newspaper!"[2]

I also distracted Yves with some of the old games we used to play with Colonel Steele. We really missed Colonel Steele, ever since he left the Yukon and went away to the Boer War in South Africa.[3]

Fortunately, Yves loves Colonel Steele's games. One is called Memory.[4] You put around twenty things on a table or chair. You get one minute to memorize them all. Then you put a towel or jacket over top and list the things underneath. The person who gets the most wins.

Another favourite is Observation. You take turns challenging the other person to remember the details of another person or place you've just been. The conductor had just walked by, so I challenged Yves to describe the conductor to me. Yves did pretty well. He got the jacket, hat, gold trim, silver whistle, key chain, black shoes and all kinds of things. But he couldn't remember whether the man had

---

2.   Editor's Note: It is interesting to speculate whether Kip really did tell Klondike millionaire Joe Boyle about his idea. Less than two years later Boyle organized the Dawson City Nuggets, including ex-Ottawa star Weldy Young. The team travelled over 4000 miles to challenge the Ottawa Silver Seven. As a Whitehorse newspaper columnist has noted, had they won they might have been the longest Stanley Cup dynasty ever (because the rules at the time said any challengers had to play on the champion team's ice and few teams would have made the trip to the Yukon!).

3.   Editor's Note: The Boer War, 1899-1902. Over 8000 Canadians served with the British Empire forces fighting the South African Republic and Boer Free State. The Boers, as they were known, were descendents of Dutch-speaking settlers in South Africa and sought to avoid being absorbed into the British Empire.

4.   Editor's Note: Colonel Steele's game "Memory" is remarkably similar to "Kim's Game" as popularized by Rudyard Kipling's novel *Kim*, in which the game is used to train the memories of young British spies in India. Since *Kim* was published in London just prior to the Alaska-Canada boundary dispute, it seems likely that Colonel Steele was playing it with Kip in the Yukon before Kipling made it world famous. Whether Steele learned it from British Intelligence on one of his foreign missions remains unknown.

a moustache or not! Sometimes you miss things that should be completely obvious. That's what makes it fun.

Yves got mad when I told him the conductor had the biggest moustache in the Yukon.

He challenged me to close my eyes and tell him all the things in our train car. You'd be surprised how hard this is. I completely missed the woodstove, which is actually the biggest thing in the whole car!

Next I challenged Yves to tell me the name of Mr. Liebherr's book without looking. To my amazement, he did. "The Strenuous Life by Theodore Roosevelt!" Yves leaned forward. "That's a pretty big book for a miner to be reading," he whispered to me.

I think Mr. Liebherr heard Yves, since he smiled. He reached in his pocket and pulled out a cloth. Inside were a sausage and some cheese. "Bierwurst, courtesy of Captain von Neidling?" he asked as he cut us a slice. It was really good. Not like those horrible English sausages Colonel Steele loves to eat. "Actually, courtesy of Captain von Neidling's cook, who has a key to his private locker." He winked at us, then started reading again.

When we got tired of the games, we just sat silently. Each of us was probably thinking about the same thing. We also listened to the men across the aisle. They were talking about the argument between Canada and Alaska over the border. They had a newspaper with a headline that said, "Alaska Boundary Dispute Flares Up." The Americans thought the border should be inland, and the Canadians and British thought it should be by the ocean.

"Think of how much gold is in between!" said one of the men.

"Worth fighting for, I reckon," said one of the others.

Eventually, though, both Yves and I drifted off to sleep.

When we got to Whitehorse, Mr. Liebherr and the conductor carried my Dad to Dr. Nicholson's new house. It's on Elliott Street so it wasn't too far[5]. Yves ran straight home to tell my sisters Aurore and Papillon and to get Maman. She's actually my stepmother but I call her Maman, which is the French word for mother. She's a very good stepmother. I don't know why every stepmother in the story books is wicked.

Dr. Nicholson gasped when he saw my Dad. I don't think doctors are supposed to do that. It made me feel really scared. We didn't even go down the street to the hospital. It was locked for the night since no one was in it. Dr. Nicholson just waved the men carrying Dad right into the kitchen.

I saw them stretch Dad out on Dr. Nicholson's kitchen table. One of my Dad's arms slipped off the side of the table and swung limply. The door was still open and I watched as Dr. Nicholson pulled Mr. Liebherr's shirt off Dad's head. There was blood everywhere. Dr. Nicholson moved quickly but carefully as he laid out his instruments. His bent down and studied Dad's injuries.

Suddenly he looked up. Our eyes met. There was a serious look on his face that both scared me and made me feel better since I knew he was working his hardest.

Then he whispered to one of the men and the door closed.

I waited in the living room for Maman to arrive. We were at the doctor's house late into the night. Finally, Dr. Nicholson came out to see us. He looked very tired.

He asked to see Maman alone in his office. I waited in the other room, kicking my heels against the chair. I got up and looked at all the bottles and medicines on the doctor's shelves. They were every possible shape and colour and had strange names like "Boric Acid" and "Chloroform." Then I noticed the doctor's fishing rod standing in the corner by the woodstove. I tried to remember some good times with my Dad, like the time we floated the boat all the way to Dawson City and fished along the way. That was the first time I caught a

---

5.   Editor's Note: In 1902 the Whitehorse Star described Dr. Nicholson commencing work "on a residence situated at the South end of town" at 208 Elliott Street. The house was called "the Doctor's House" for many years as a series of doctors made it home. It is now known as the Mast House. Visitors on Whitehorse's Heritage Buildings walking tour can see the building in a new location on Wood Street.

pike all by myself. Or the first time Dad and I met Aurore and Yves on Lake Bennett.

I felt a hot tear trickle down my cheek and drop onto the floor.

All of a sudden, the door to the kitchen opened. "Kip, your mother's English lessons with Mr. Galpin don't seem to have taken. I guess you'll have to translate."

I gulped and went in. Maman was sitting on a wooden chair in the corner. She was crying. It was strange, but she looked very small. I suddenly remembered that her first husband had died before she moved to the Yukon.

When she saw me, she stood up, sniffed and straightened her dress. She seemed more like herself again. Then she reached out and put her hand on my shoulder.

"Sois fort," she said softly. She looked me in the eye and gave my shoulder a squeeze. Be strong.

I would try.

The doctor thought Dad was going to survive, but I could tell he wasn't sure. But he would be laid up in bed for several weeks at least. That's when I started to cry. I couldn't help myself. I sniffed and tried to stop.

I asked Maman in French how we would pay the doctor's bills. She said we had money for the doctor. But she didn't know how we were going to pay the bank. Dad had just borrowed a lot of money from the bank to buy our boat and fix it up. Now it was at the bottom of Lake Bennett. Maman also told me that the boat didn't have any insurance, which is where you pay the insurance company a little bit each year and they buy you a new boat if there's an accident. I guess the insurance company thought a Yukon river boat was too risky and wouldn't sell Dad an insurance policy. And our house had a mortgage, which meant we owed the bank money for it too. If we didn't pay, they could take our house away.

Dr. Nicholson waited quietly until we were done talking, then suggested we go home and come back the next morning.

We walked home in silence. I didn't know what to say.

It wasn't until we got home that I was able to talk. "Maman," I said, "I'll get a job. Mr. Carruthers at the White Horse Hotel said I could carry bags there."

Maman smiled a little bit and put her arm around me. "Tu es comme ton papa," she said. You're like your father. Somehow, that made me feel a little bit better.

Chapter 3

Colonel Sam Steele Returns!

"Alaska Border Dispute: 3 American, 2 Canadian and 1 British Judge to form Independent Tribunal in London"

—Newspaper story from my scrapbook
June 17, 1903

It was one of those fine Yukon summer days when you feel sorry for all the people who live Outside[1]. There were no clouds and the sky was a brilliant blue. You could feel the sun warm your skin, but it wasn't too hot. The smell of the lodgepole pines was in the air and the light was so clear I could see the grayling darting around in my favourite fishing spot in the Yukon River.

For a minute, it made me forget that my Dad was in the hospital. If only I had been more careful with those boxes! Did one of them have dynamite in it? Or what if I hadn't dropped the boxes? Dad might have been in the boat or somewhere else when the explosion happened!

Rudi said it was my fault. Mr. Liebherr hadn't said anything about it, but then again he was too nice to ever tell me that it was my fault. But he probably thought it.

---

1.   Editor's Note: "Outside" is Yukon slang still used today to mean anywhere not in the Yukon, from Venezuela to Vancouver.

I'd been thinking about that a lot. The night before, I lay in my bed in the dark for ages trying to remember exactly what happened.

"Are you sad?" asked Yves out of nowhere. We were walking to school at the time. He always knows your feelings somehow.

"No!" I said. I kicked a rock. It bounced off a post right into Yves's shin. He started to cry. "It wasn't my fault!" I shouted. "Stupid post."

Why did things always go like that? It just wasn't fair. I kicked another rock.

Above: The White Horse Hotel where Kip carried luggage. The von Neidlings' room was in the back on the upper floor. (Photo courtesy of MacBride Museum 1999-251-191)

School didn't go very well that day.

It started with math. Mr. Galpin was writing on the blackboard. Mr. Galpin had moved me to the front of the class since he said I needed to work on paying attention.

I could hear Rudi whispering just behind me. He was making little "boom" noises and pretending to blow things up on his desk. I looked back and he had a little drawing of a boat with "Kip" and "Kip's Dad" on it.

"Kip, turn around and pay attention!" snapped Mr. Galpin.

Rudi put up his hand. "Mr. Galpin, sir, can you show us that long division trick you taught us last week?" Mr. Galpin smiled. He loved math. Rudi was, as usual, sucking up.

As Mr. Galpin turned to the board and began explaining it, Rudi leaned forward. "Dad blower-upper! It was your fault—"

Before he could finish, I leapt out of my chair and was on top of him.

Mr. Galpin hauled me off and slung me into the corner.

Rudi lay on the floor. He was pretending to be hurt. I hadn't even had time to punch him. "Mr. Galpin," he moaned. "Please help me. I don't want to miss math." What an actor! I couldn't believe Mr. Galpin believed him!

"Kip, explain yourself!" said Mr. Galpin. His eyes were narrow and his nostrils were twitching. He was mad!

But what was I supposed to say? That Rudi said I'd blown up my own father? When it might even—probably was—true? I looked down at my feet.

"Unacceptable, Kip." Mr. Galpin grabbed my ear and lifted me out of the corner. Still pulling my ear, he marched me over to his desk. I tried to stand on my tip-toes so my ear wouldn't hurt so much, but he just pulled higher.

The ear pull was one of Mr. Galpin's standard punishments. But the thing I really didn't like was the strap. At least he didn't use a cane like some teachers, but I still hated the strap.

He rummaged around in his desk for his favourite leather belt, muttering that poem of his: "O ye who teach the ingenious youth of nations, I pray ye flog them upon all occasions."[2]

At least it's more original than our substitute teachers, who all seem to say, "Spare the rod, spoil the child."

I clenched my teeth. Mr. Galpin hit me three times, hard. Then he made me stand in front of the class and show them the red marks on my hands. Believe it or not, that was the worst part. Then he sent me home.

I can tell you, Maman wasn't too pleased to see me.

I sat in my room all afternoon. Gosh, Rudi made me mad.

I would have been grounded for weeks if I didn't have my after school job.

Since my Dad got hurt, I had a couple of jobs. I cut wood. I delivered messages for the Telegraph Office on Front Street. But my main job was at the White Horse Hotel. I came down whenever a boat or train came in and helped carry the bags from the station across Front Street to the hotel. The work was hard but Mr. Carruthers paid me fairly. If there were a lot of travellers, I could make more than a dollar a day.[3]

The only trouble was that Captain von Neidling and Rudi lived in the hotel, so Rudi got a chance to make fun of me every day.

I don't know why they lived in a hotel. I suppose Captain von Neidling was pretty rich. Anyway, they had moved right in. I helped the maid clean the rooms sometimes and their room was full of pictures

---

2.   Editor's Note: Mr. Galpin is quoting English poet Lord Byron: "O ye who teach the ingenuous youth of nations—/Holland, France, England, Germany or Spain;/I pray ye flog them upon all occasions, It mends their morals—never mind the pain." Note Kip's confusion between the words "ingenious" and "ingenuous."

3.   Editor's Note: At the time, an adult labourer in the Yukon could earn $5–10 per day depending on the type of work. Kip's dollar did go farther than today, with a loaf of bread costing around 5¢ and raisins about 10¢/pound. Luxuries like chocolate were much more expensive, often more than 30¢ per bar.

of Africa and relatives in Germany. Captain von Neidling even had his old sword from the navy in the closet!

Above: Colonel Sam Steele of the Yukon. (Photo courtesy of MacBride Museum 1989-1-199)

Yves usually came along too when I went to meet the boats. He was too little to carry heavy suitcases, but he helped old ladies across the street and generally acted cute.

Usually the old ladies would tip him more than they did me.

Anyway, we were walking up Main Street counting the nickels we had earned when Yves pulled my sleeve. "Hey! That man walks like Colonel Sam Steele!" Other kids in town called him "Sam," but for some reason Yves always called him "Colonel Sam Steele." That is, that's what Yves called Colonel Steele before he left the country on his mission to Africa.

Yves tapped me on the arm again and pointed at a tall, broad shouldered man in a brand new overcoat and a fancy, big city hat. D'Artagnan gave a little woof as if he recognized the man too.

I looked more carefully. Yves was right. The man took long strides like he was used to walking and he stood up perfectly straight. Anyone who's ever met Colonel Steele will know that he doesn't slouch!

In fact, you don't slouch when you're around him either.

Yves and I dodged a couple of horses in the street and crossed to follow the man. I think he heard our footsteps, because he stopped and pretended to look in a shop window. He glanced backwards down the sidewalk. We met his eyes.

"Colonel Sam Steele!" shouted Yves. He raced forward and hugged one of Colonel Steele's huge thighs.

"Damn!" said Sam Steele with a sigh. "I was supposed to be here incognito."[4] He smiled and ruffled my hair like he used to. Then he picked Yves up.

"What does 'incognito' mean?" asked Yves.

---

4.   Editor's note: Prior to this, historians had believed that Sam Steele was on duty at this time in South Africa, where he commanded Division B of the South African Constabulary after the Boer War ended. His return to the Yukon is not recorded in any official records, although—strangely—there are no confirmed reports of him in South Africa during the Alaska-Canada boundary dispute either! Perhaps future releases of declassified documents in London will shed further light on this matter.

"Disguised," said Colonel Steele.

Yves laughed and poked Sam Steele in the chest. "Hiding Sam Steele in the Yukon would be like hiding a moose on Main Street!"

We made him promise to come to our house for dinner that night. He agreed. "I'd love a moose steak, especially if your mother is cooking it," he declared. "I've eaten nothing but wildebeest and antelope for months!"

Suddenly, he seemed distracted. I followed his eyes. He was look-ing at a man who had just said "Good day" and walked past us on the sidewalk.

Sam crouched down. "Boys, don't look. But what did you notice about that fellow that just walked past?"

He said it playfully like he was playing one of his old games with us. But I sensed he wasn't playing this time.

"He walks like you," said Yves. "Big steps. No slouching!"

"And all his clothes are new. His hat isn't faded at all. And his shoes aren't scuffed," I said.

"So you think he's a cheechako?" [5]

"No," I said. "Somehow he looks like he knows what he's doing. Plus his face is tanned like he's outside all the time. It's just that his clothes are new like yours. I think he's on vacation from the army or something."

Sam smiled. "What about his accent? Whose army?"

"American," I said.

"Do you know who he is?"

I remembered carrying the man's suitcases. "He's staying at the White Horse Hotel. Been there about ten days. His suitcases are

---

5.   Editor's Note: A cheechako is a newcomer to the North. The word comes from Chinook Wawa, or what used to be called Chinook Jar-gon. The MacBride Museum's historical experts tell us that Chinook Jar-gon is a trade language that was used on the Pacific Coast in the 19th and early 20th centuries, by both Europeans and First Nations. A long-time resident of the Yukon or Alaska is known as a sourdough.

brand new too. And he's got a huge camera case. I could barely lift it!"

"What does he do every day?"

"He travels around Whitehorse, or takes trips on the train or rivers with his camera. He seems like he's on holidays, but by himself. I've seen him walking by the railway making lots of notes in his note-book."

"I heard him ask one of your men how many policemen there were in the Yukon," said Yves.

"Did he now?" Sam said slowly, rubbing his chin.

Colonel Steele was thinking about this when another man came up to us.

"Hello, Percy," said Colonel Steele, almost with a sigh. He didn't seem all that happy to see the man.

"Colonel Steele, I thought you were supposed to be incognito," said Percy, not even saying hello to us. He had a fancy English accent like the King's.

He ignored us until Yves pointed at him and said, "You're the Pic-cadilly Dude from the Ice Worm Cocktail!"[6] Percy's jaw dropped. Yves turned to me in excitement. "You should have seen Joe Boyle tell him off on the Chilkoot Pass!"[7]

Percy pulled himself together and gave us a nasty look. It was a look I got to know well later. It meant something like "kids are stupid, and kids from the colonies are even worse." He was one of those

---

6.   Editor's Note: Major Percy Brown is well known as the arrogant and ridiculous "Piccadilly Dude" in Robert Service's *The Ballad of the Ice Worm Cocktail*. In it, grizzled Yukon miners in the Malamute Saloon tell Percy that he will be become a real sourdough if he drinks a cocktail with an "ice worm" in it. After he forces down the worm and staggers out of the saloon, it turns out that the ice worm was just a piece of spa-ghetti with red spots for eyes. What is relatively unknown, however, is that by 1903 Percy was attached to the British Embassy in Washington and appears to have been a member of British Intelligence.

7.   Editor's Note: Yves's first encounter with Percy is described In *Aurore of the Yukon*.

English people who think everything English is superior to anything in the New World.

"I don't have time for children's stories," said Percy with a sniff. "We have business to do."

I could tell Yves was about to say "What business?" But Percy turned on his heel and stomped off down the sidewalk.

The three of us watched Percy walk away. "He walks like a cheechako," said Yves.

"Yep," agreed Sam Steele.

Chapter 4

A Spy in the Yukon?

======================================

"The U.S. Army isn't in Alaska to pick blueberries!"

—*Colonel Sam Steele, in my journal*
June 18, 1903

Yves and I rushed home to tell Maman we had invited Colonel Steele over for dinner. Usually, we would have gotten in trouble for inviting someone over without asking. But Maman was excited to see Colonel Steele again too. I helped my sister Aurore get the big dinner table ready. Yves set the fireplace for a big fire, even though it was June. My other sister Papillon started to make duff for dessert. She went down to the cellar to get our last jar of blueberry jam from the summer before to put on top.

We got even more excited when a note arrived from Colonel Steele asking if he could invite Percy and "Mr. Ricardo."

"Why is 'Mr. Ricardo' in quotation marks?" asked Aurore.

Colonel Steele didn't tell us right away when he arrived. First he complimented my sisters on their dresses, told Yves and me that we looked "dashing" in our Sunday clothes and told my mother the house looked wonderful. He had even visited Dad in the hospital and said that he looked fit enough to hike the Chilkoot. We all knew this wasn't really true. But it was nice. He was always a very polite visitor. He even said "Bonsoir" to my mother. She really liked that. She still barely speaks any English. We mostly speak French at home, but all of us kids speak English at school and around town.

He also brought a gift for the family: a book called *Kim* by a fellow named Rudyard Kipling. It was about a boy in India and had come out in London the year before. Colonel Steele always liked to bring us things that we could learn from.

Only then did he tell us about the quotation marks. "I don't think Mr. Ricardo is his real name. I went digging around this afternoon after I saw you boys. I suspect that his real name is Captain Wilds P. Richardson. That's the name of the man in charge of the new United States Army base at Fort Seward near Haines, not too far from Skagway."[1]

"There aren't army soldiers in Alaska!" exclaimed Yves.

"Of course there are," replied Aurore. "President Roosevelt sent them there in case there's a war over the border between Alaska and the Yukon, right Colonel Steele?" Aurore smiled proudly. She loves reading the newspapers and telling us all about it. She borrows the London paper from Mr. Taylor at Taylor & Drury's general store, even though it is usually weeks or months old by the time it gets to Whitehorse.

"Yep," said Colonel Steele. "The president sent 800 soldiers to Alaska. They're building a big fort at Haines. You heard what President Roosevelt said: 'Walk softly and carry a big stick.' He's trying to remind us that he means business about the border. Just like he did a few months ago when he threatened to send in the U.S. Navy if the German Navy didn't stop bombarding Venezuela."[2]

---

1.   Editor's Note: This is remarkable new evidence of U.S. Army preparation for a potential war with Canada. Captain (later General) Wilds P. Richardson was a famous frontier soldier in Alaska. In addition to building Fort Seward at Haines, he also surveyed the Valdez-Fairbanks road (later renamed the Richardson Highway). In 1908, he ordered his men to find and open a trail through the Iditarod country to Nome, Alaska. This, of course, came be known as the famous "Iditarod Trail." Today, U.S. Army headquarters in Alaska is located at Fort Richardson near Anchorage.

"L'armée américaine! Est-ce qu'une guerre est vraiment possible?" asked Maman in French.

"Yes, ma'am, I'm afraid a war is possible. More possible than you think! The U.S. Army isn't in Alaska to pick blueberries!" said Colonel Steele. "It's why the president sent soldiers to Alaska. Same reason we had the Yukon Field Force at Fort Selkirk down the Yukon River. Although that was only 200 men and they've all gone home now. You know, there was almost a war between Britain and America just eight years ago. That was a border dispute too! The Venezuela-Guyana border, believe it or not. It's too complicated to get into, but Guyana is a British colony like Canada and the Americans were on Venezuela's side. President Roosevelt wasn't president yet, but he said a war with Britain would be a great chance for the United States to capture Canada!"

"But why are they arguing over the border?" I asked. "When we go to Skagway, the border is marked right at the top of the White Pass!"

"That's just the temporary border. No one can agree where the real border is between Canada and the Alaskan Panhandle.[3] Canada says that Skagway should be part of Canada. The Americans say the mountains and Lake Bennett should be in Alaska. The prob-

---

2.   Editor's Note: Steele is referring to the Venezuela war scare of 1902/03. After Venezuela defaulted on its debts, several European countries sent warships to pressure the Venezuelan dictator. The German Navy was particularly aggressive, raising worries in Roosevelt's White House that they intended to seize a permanent base there as they had done in China a few years before. Roosevelt is said to have warned the German ambassador that he would order Admiral Dewey's fleet to attack the German ships if they continued to attack Venezuela.

3.   Editor's Note: The Alaskan Panhandle is the part of the state that stretches down the Pacific Coast. On the map, it appears like a "handle" connected to the main part of Alaska (the "pan"). Colonel Steele is characteristically modest about his role. He was the one who set the provisional border in 1898, since the Canadian government needed somewhere to set up customs posts and collect duties from gold seekers headed to Dawson City.

lem is this old treaty that was signed when Russia still owned Alaska. Believe it or not, none of the people who signed it had ever even been to Alaska. And they didn't have very good maps. So the wording of the treaty is very confusing! Plus it's in French and Russian. So it's quite a mess!"

There was a knock at the door. Percy introduced himself. He spoke very nice European French. But you could tell he didn't think much of our house. Not many houses in London are made of logs!

"Mr. Ricardo" arrived just a few minutes later. We had a very nice dinner. Even Yves sat in his chair and listened to the talk. Only Percy was moody. He sat at one end of the table looking sour like he wished he was in a fancy restaurant in London. Nobody said anything about the border argument. That would have been impolite.

It turned out that "Mr. Ricardo" had met President Theodore Roosevelt. Actually, he was a huge fan of "TR," as he called the president. He even gave me a photo for my scrapbook. So we asked him all kinds of questions.

"Well, TR is a great man," said "Mr. Ricardo." "When you meet him, he just fills the room with energy. Mental and physical. He reads 2 or 3 books a day, swims in the Potomac River every morning. He's written 10 books and passed all kinds of laws. He says he's going to give every American a chance for a 'square deal' so he's been standing up to the big railway and oil companies."

"Why do they call him a 'Rough Rider?'" asked my sister Aurore. Like I said, she's always reading the newspaper.

"Because when the war with Spain started five years ago, he quit his fancy job in Washington and organized more than a thousand men to join the U.S. Army. Their official name was the 1st Volunteer Cavalry, but everyone called them the 'Rough Riders.' Their most famous battle was in Cuba, when TR led them up San Juan Hill. He was a national hero after that!"

"Mr. Ricardo" was so excited he could hardly stop talking about TR.

"Est-ce qu'il va vous visiter en Alaska?" asked Maman. Papillon translated this and "Mr. Ricardo" nearly jumped out of his chair in excitement.

"We've invited him. TR sure would love Alaska. He's written books on wildlife, hunting and adventure. Alaska's got it all! Plus he loves to hunt. And I sure would like to show him all the places we need roads and bridges and ports. He'd get the money for us. But now that he's president, it's tough to go camping. So many newspapermen follow him around! One time, he went bear hunting in the Lower 48[4] and there were so many people following him in the woods that a journalist actually stepped on his foot!"

It was very fun to have such interesting people over for dinner. We all felt kind of strange doing it with Dad in the hospital. On the one hand, he had to be in the hospital and would have wanted us to be happy. On the other, I felt really guilty being happy when he was so hurt.

We finished our main course and took a break while Maman got dessert ready. Percy and Colonel Steele went out into the backyard to get some fresh air. Mr. Ricardo sat down in the living room.

Meanwhile, we carried the plates into the kitchen. Before Dad's accident, Maman had been saving up to get more plates so we could have separate ones for dinner and dessert. But in the meantime they had to be washed and used again.

Aurore pulled my sleeve and whispered into my ear. "I'm going to sit in the living room with 'Mr. Ricardo' and try to find out more about why he's in the Yukon."

"Good idea. See if you can find out if he really is Captain Richardson," I said. I watched as she sat down beside "Mr. Ricardo" and asked him how he was enjoying his trip to the Yukon.

I listened as he explained how much he loved beautiful mountains, wide rivers and so on. "Mr. Ricardo" looked relaxed as he ram-

---

4.   Editor's Note: Lower 48 is Alaskan slang for the 48 southern states of the United States.

bled on. Even though you could tell it wasn't the whole story, Aurore just smiled politely and listened.

Then I felt a tap on my shoulder. It was Maman holding out a dish towel for me. "But it's Aurore's turn!" I said in surprise. Then I realized. Maman would never call Aurore into the kitchen if she was keeping a guest company and I was just standing around in the kitchen.

"Ha ha!" laughed Yves. "Aurore outsmarted Soapy Smith and now she's outsmarted you!"

He was right. Maman tossed the towel onto my shoulder with a smile.

Above: Whitehorse in 1903. Note the White Horse Hotel, Arctic Restaurant and train tracks Kip described in the story. (Photo courtesy of MacBride Museum 1989-4-312)

I gritted my teeth and started drying. Yves was still smirking. "Hey Yves, you better get some more dishes off the table," I said. "Papillon has disappeared too!" My little brother's smile disappeared, but mine came back a little bit.

After drying five or six plates, I took the opportunity to carry them back out to the table for dessert. Each time, I could hear a little of what Aurore and "Mr. Ricardo" were talking about.

Aurore was asking him a question. "If this is your big vacation, Mr. Ricardo, why didn't you bring your wife and family?"

"Mr. Ricardo" looked a bit nervous all of a sudden. "Err, my wife doesn't like to travel in the back country."

"But you said she loved Alaska," replied Aurore innocently. I smiled to myself and went back to the kitchen.

When I was done my next batch of plates, I heard another of Aurore's questions. "Why do you take so many pictures of railroads and sternwheelers?" Mr. Ricardo was looking even more nervous than before.

Finally, I finished the plates and brought the last ones out for dessert. I was just in time to hear Aurore say, "Would you like some tea, Captain Richardson?"

"Why yes I would, thank you," he replied. He smiled for a second until he realized she had called him "Captain Richardson" and not "Mr. Ricardo." "Err, Aurore," he stuttered. "don't you mean 'Mr. Ricardo'?"

"Oh, sorry Mr. Ricardo," said Aurore. "Just a slip of the tongue."

After I was done the plates, I really wanted to go outside and tell Colonel Steele about Captain Richardson. But Maman shooed me back into the kitchen to help her with the duff. We put the jam in the bottom of the bowl, poured the duff batter on top and carefully put it in a pot of boiling water. I usually love making the duff since our family rule was that you got the first piece if you helped make it. But not that night. Instead, I desperately wished I was in the backyard with Colonel Steele.

After the duff was on the stove, I trudged up the stairs. I had to put our carving knife back in the wooden case under Maman's dresser and get our dessert spoons. I wondered bitterly why it always seemed to be me doing the chores.

Then, out the open window, I saw Papillon's smile and big blue eyes twinkling at me through the leaves in the trembling aspen in our backyard. She loved to climb it and hide high up in the branches.

I was about to shout "Get in here and dry some dishes!" when she suddenly put her finger in front of her lips and pointed down.

Colonel Steele and Percy were right underneath her. She was listening in!

Above: A sketch by Papillon found in Kip's scrapbook, showing her secretly listening to Colonel Steele and Percy in the backyard.

I also saw why they wanted to go outside. They were smoking cigars. The smoke was rising up into the tree and making Papillon wrinkle her nose.

I dumped the knife on the bed and moved to the window. Percy was telling Colonel Steele about London. "Now, Steele, I hope we won't offend our hostess. In London it's absolutely *de rigeur* to wait until after dessert to smoke. Typically the ladies retire to the drawing room while the men—"

"Never mind London," replied Colonel Steele. "We have to talk about our American friend and I know he doesn't smoke."

"Oh right. I see. Of course, the smoking's just a stratagem. I was with you from the start," replied Percy. "Now how do you know this American fellow's been taking photographs of the railway?"

"A source at the hotel," replied Colonel Steele. I wondered who else at the hotel besides me he had been talking to. No one else had paid much attention to "Mr. Ricardo."

"A source!" exclaimed Percy excitedly. "Spiffo! I've been trying to recruit a source ever since I got here! London will be happy to hear that we have a source. We'll call him Agent 'Y1.'"

Colonel Steele smiled. "Actually, he's just a—"

But Percy interrupted him. "Don't tell me who he is in public! Security, Steele! You must remember that security is paramount!" Paramount is a fancy word that means "really important." Percy looked over his shoulder as if to see if anyone was hiding in our rhubarb patch.

Papillon sat perfectly still while Percy stepped nervously around D'Artagnan's doghouse and looked over our fence. Only her eyelid moved as she winked at me.

Colonel Steele didn't seem to notice her either. He looked both annoyed and amused for some reason. "All right. Anyway, my source ... I mean Y1 ... yes, Y1 told me that he's been here about 10 days. He's got all new clothes, hat, boots. He spends his days taking pictures and making notes about rivers, railways, steamboats and so on."

"Egad!" said Percy. "Egad" is a world that fancy English people use instead of "holy smokes!" I was amazed too, since I had told Colonel Steele the same thing!

"Exactly," said Colonel Steele. "He's scouting out the Yukon in case the U.S. Army attacks. It's exactly what I'd do if I were him."

"But he's not being very secret about it. I mean, the camera, the new clothes. And picking a secret name like 'Ricardo' when your real name is Richardson. These Americans don't seem very clever," snorted Percy.

"I don't know about that," said Colonel Steele. "Maybe he wants us to know he's spying on us so we'll report it to London."

"Why would he do that?"

"Like President Roosevelt says, 'Walk softly and carry a big stick.' I bet the Americans want to scare us into giving them everything they want in London."

"Oh! Yes! I understand now ... I mean, just as I was thinking!" replied Percy. "I'll report Y1's message to London right away. I'll write it upstairs here. Did you say that blond boy was a messenger for the Telegraph Office? He doesn't look *too* dim. I suppose he could deliver it."

I heard Maman's voice. "Le dessert!" I looked guiltily at the carving knife lying on Maman's bed. Colonel Steele looked guiltily at his cigar.

I put the carving knife back, grabbed the spoons and dashed downstairs.

Everyone was sitting around the table waiting for the duff. Colonel Steele was telling everyone about the time he made a duff in the bush with the batter inside a tobacco tin being boiled on a campfire inside a bucket.

Anyway, the duff turned out perfectly. Maman took the pot out of the boiling water and turned it upside down. Out slid the duff. The Yukon blueberry jam was steaming and oozing deliciously down from the top. We poured canned milk on top. It was delicious. Even Percy liked it. "Madame, c'est une merveille bucolique!" he exclaimed.

"What is a 'mer-vey boo-kol-eek' in English?" asked Colonel Steele.

"Why, a bucolic marvel of course!" replied Percy.

Colonel Steele thought about this for a minute. "Hmm ... if that means 'a very fine duff,' then I couldn't agree more!"

After that, Maman sent us upstairs to our bedroom while the adults stayed in the living room. Dad had said that if things went well with his new boat, we might be able to afford a bigger house with separate bedrooms for the girls and Yves and me. But since our boat was at the bottom of Bennett Lake, the four of us were stuck sharing a room.

At least Yves and I had bunk beds. The girls had to share.

Aurore poked her head out from under the covers. "Who is this secret agent Y1?" she whispered.

We all thought about this for a minute.

Then Papillon's head popped up. "I think it's Kip!"

But before we could say anything else, Maman opened the door. Percy was right beside her with a piece of paper in his hand. "Boy!" he called. "Run this message to the Telegraph Office. Wake them up. It's urgent for London!"

I jumped into my boots, tossed my hockey sweater over my pyjamas, grabbed one more bite of duff in the kitchen and sprinted for the Telegraph Office with D'Artagnan barking at my heels.

Above: The Whitehorse streets Kip ran down with Percy's message. This photo shows some of his friends on Second Avenue, beside Mr. Taylor's yard. (Photo courtesy of Bill & Aline Taylor collection)

Chapter 5

Burglary in Dead Horse Gulch

"Train Robbery! Famous Lawman Sam Steele Ripped Off"

—*The Skagway News*
June 23, 1903

Life went back to normal pretty quickly after dinner with Colonel Steele, Percy and "Mr. Ricardo."

Unfortunately, "normal" wasn't very much fun. We would go to school and then go to our jobs. I was getting pretty sick of carrying suitcases. And every telegram I delivered seemed to be urgent. I was constantly running up and down Main Street.

The good news was that Dad was home. We were so excited when Maman told us he was coming. For some reason, we all thought he would be better.

We were shocked when they brought him into the house in a stretcher! He wasn't better yet. Maman just couldn't afford to have him stay at the hospital any more.

Still, we were so glad to have him around. We all felt a bit better since we could get him cups of tea or help Maman put on clean bandages. Aurore would read to him from the newspaper and I would tell him about everything going on around town. His head still had a huge bandage and his leg was in a cast. When Dr. Nicholson visited, you could tell he was still worried.

Dad slept a lot. He was very pale, like there was no blood under his skin. But sometimes he was awake. Then he would smile a little bit for you. He was pretty confused. "The boat needs paint," he would say. "Or winter's coming. Better chop some wood." It was scary to see Dad like that, to tell you the truth. Dr. Nicholson said it was because of the medicine he was taking. I noticed that no matter how you asked, Dr. Nicholson would never say when he thought Dad would get better.

Maman had so many jobs I couldn't keep track. She was working extra hard since Dad was still in the hospital. Maman cooked at the Regina Hotel. She also helped in one of the shops on Main Street. After we went to bed, she sewed hems and fixed clothes for Taylor & Drury. And in her spare time, she baked bread which Yves delivered around town in his wagon!

Maman was out of the house a lot when she was working. At first it was kind of fun to be able to do whatever we wanted. But it got sad pretty fast. I never realized all the things she did for us like inventing games, making snacks and generally keeping the house happy. And not only that, but my best friend Jack was away too. His summer job was as ship's boy on the sternwheeler S.S. Canadian.

Aurore was working in Mr. Taylor's store in the ladies shoes and clothes department. She had to fold the clothes after customers tried them on.

Papillon took care of Mrs. Liebherr's two-year-old baby while Yves walked Mrs. Liebherr's dog. The Liebherrs lived in a tiny shack with just two rooms behind the Taylor & Drury warehouse near the river. Mrs. Liebherr was always there and it's not as if she was ever more than 10 feet from the baby. So I don't know if she really needed help. I think she was just pretending to need help so Maman didn't have to take care of Papillon and Yves.

As for Yves, he would also take his wagon and run down to Front Street. He'd go to Taylor & Drury's, the hotels, just about anywhere and ask if they needed anything delivered. Then he'd load whatever it was into his wagon and roll away. Everybody thinks Yves is cute. They never shut up about his "twinkling brown eyes." I think people sometimes asked him to deliver things just to see him smile and toddle down the road with his wagon.

I can't figure it out. If there's any kind of twinkle in my eye, it just seems to make people want to ground me or shout at me.

Anyway, living in a small town is good sometimes. It seemed like everybody in Whitehorse had brought over an apple pie or a fresh loaf of bread. Mr. Liebherr would come over and help me chop wood for the stove sometimes. We would always offer him some of Maman's bread, but if he took any he would always be back the next day with German black rye bread that he called "pumpernickel," or sometimes with pickled cabbage called "sauerkraut."

My Dad's friends from out in the bush helped us too. One day, a native boy named Louie dropped by with fresh grayling from the Yukon River. I remembered him from a trip with my Dad and Mr. Taylor to Teslin the summer before. He won the Teslin bike race while we were there.

It's kind of surprising that Teslin has a bike race, since they don't really have any roads. In fact, no one in Whitehorse would believe it until they saw a picture Mr. Taylor took!

Anyway, I think my Dad ran into Louie's father on a dog sled trip up the Teslin River one winter and helped him out somehow. It was really nice of Louie and his father to bring grayling since I didn't have time to fish much anymore.

Every evening, when the chores were done, we would sit with Dad. You expect your Dad to always be strong and full of energy. We all tried to smile when we sat with him. But I couldn't help thinking that he would have been somewhere else if I hadn't messed up with those boxes.

We were all pretty glum.

Above: A bike race in Teslin like the one described by Kip. (Photo courtesy of the Bill & Aline Taylor collection)

I think that's why Maman didn't cancel our trip to Skagway. Papillon had won our whole family train tickets by guessing exactly when the ice in Dawson City would break up. Spring Break-up in Dawson City is pretty exciting since the ice usually whooshes away all at once. They have a contest every year. You have to guess exactly what minute the ice goes out.

All the sourdoughs laughed at Papillon when she picked the last day of April. Break up is always in May, they said. I told her to pick a time in May. But Papillon just smiled and bought her ticket.

Everyone was pretty surprised when the ice went out in April and Papillon won the prize!

So Maman told Mr. Galpin at school that we would miss a day. Mrs. Liebherr said she would check on Dad. We got up early and went down to the train station. The train stops at Bennett halfway to Skagway for a lunch of baked beans. We also took a picnic basket since it was too expensive to buy food on the train. And we took the book Colonel Steele given us, *Kim*. The train takes eight hours so a book is a good idea.

We were pretty excited to be going to Skagway. It's always fun there. Plus everyone treats us really well because of how Aurore and Yves helped them get rid of Soapy Smith.[1]

But we were even more excited when we got to the station because Colonel Steele was going to be on our train too. We hadn't seen much of him. He was busy going through old files at the North West Mounted Police post. He also went down to Dawson City to go through the Commissioner's Archives. Aurore figured he was looking for papers about the border to take back to London.

"Why else would Percy come along with him? Percy works at the British Embassy in Washington, D.C., so he's got to be involved in the boundary dispute," she said.

She's usually right about this kind of thing.

The conductor made us put our dog D'Artagnan in the baggage car, despite Papillon arguing that he was a member of the family. After that, we went to find Colonel Steele on the platform while we waited to get on the train. Soon he was telling us about a huge grizzly bear he saw on the banks of the river on his way to Dawson City. Then we noticed Percy.

He didn't walk up to us. His back was to us, but he was inching towards Colonel Steele. When he was close, he pretended still not to see us but turned his head and whispered something to Colonel Steele. I couldn't hear it.

But Yves did. "What documents?" he said very loudly. "In that briefcase?" he asked, pointing at the leather case in Colonel Steele's hands.

Percy jumped like someone had stuck a red hot fireplace poker into his leg. "Shhh!" he hissed at Yves. Then he walked quickly away.

Colonel Steele patted Yves on the head. "Yes," he replied quietly. I couldn't tell if he was smiling because he thought Yves was funny, or because Percy was.

---

1.   Editor's note: The involvement of Aurore and Yves in the famous Soapy Smith shoot-out in Skagway is described in *Aurore of the Yukon*.

Above: A White Pass & Yukon Route train like the one Kip rode with Colonel Steele. Note the bridge and steep cliffs.(Photo courtesy of MacBride Museum 1989-9-019).

Then it was time to get on the train. "Is that Black Moran?" whispered Aurore in my ear. It was hard to tell. If it was, he'd shaved his famous black whiskers and got a new hat.

We got on the train and got our seats. The chairs on the train flip backward and forward so you can always get a good view. I could see Aurore watching the fellow she thought was Black Moran. He had flipped his seat to face backwards away from us, which was kind of strange since everyone wants to be looking forward if they can. The view of the mountains is fantastic.

The train ride is always lots of fun. First we sat on the left side to see the river. Then the right side to see Lake Bennett. We rode in the car, then we went outside onto the platform. The conductor took us to the caboose at the back of the train and showed us how everything worked. We had a huge lunch of Yukon baked beans in Bennett, then we got back on the train.

The best part of the trip is from the Summit down to Skagway. You won't believe the mountains until you see them. The train tracks are literally cut into the rocks along the edge of cliffs. Waterfalls splash down onto the train and get you wet if you're on the platform out-side.

At the Summit, Colonel Steele showed us where he put the North West Mounted Police tent marking the border back in 1898. Then we began to rattle downhill towards Tunnel Mountain and Dead Horse Gulch. Tunnel Mountain has that name because it has the longest train tunnel in the United States. Dead Horse Gulch is a very steep valley where hundreds of horses died on the slippery trails during the Gold Rush. Everyone was in such a hurry to get to Dawson City that they didn't take very good care of their horses.

My ears popped as we went into the tunnel. Everyone on the train said "oooh!" like they always do. It was pitch black. The train made one of its usual lurches and I felt somebody brush past me in the dark. Who would be silly enough to walk around on a White Pass train in the dark as it rattled side to side on bent rails?

Yves grabbed my arm. He doesn't like pitch black. And Tunnel Mountain is a long tunnel.

Finally, we caught a glimmer of light reflecting of the wet rock walls and then we were back out in the open. Everybody said "oooh!" again since the tunnel comes straight out of a cliff face onto a bridge hundreds of feet in the air.

Suddenly, there was a shriek from Yves. "A briefcase!" I jumped to the window, just in time to see a brown blur disappear like a rocket into the forest a hundred feet below. "That looked just like Colonel Steele's new briefcase!" said Yves. "I saw it fly through the air!"

Everyone laughed for a moment. Then we all looked up to the rack where Colonel Steele had put his briefcase. There was just a gap between Percy's suitcase and Maman's.

"Black Moran's seat is empty!" shouted Aurore.

"Black Moran!" barked Colonel Steele. He jumped up from his seat.

"Somebody brushed by me in the tunnel," I said and pointed. "Headed that way!"

Colonel Steele strode to the end of the car, whipped open the door, and stepped across the gap into the next car. We all followed. Black Moran was sitting facing the door with the Dawson City Nugget newspaper open on his lap.

"Black Moran!" shouted Colonel Steele. You could tell he was mad!

Black Moran looked up calmly. "Envy and wrath shorten the life, Colonel. Ecclesiasticus 30:24," he said. His voice was rough and raspy. I've heard the bank manager in Whitehorse describe it as "bedrock grit."[2] He pulled his jacket to the side so we could all see his pistol. "Welcome to the United States. If I recall, you're just a Canadian policeman." He smiled.

Colonel Steele understood in a moment. "I can't arrest him, kids. We're not in Canada. And I've got no evidence. No doubt a buddy of his was waiting in Dead Horse Gulch and is long gone with my briefcase."

Black Moran smiled. "Top of the day to you!" He tipped his hat in fake politeness and picked up his newspaper again.

I noticed Captain von Neidling sitting at the far end of the car. He was watching us like a cat.

We closed the door to Black Moran's car. While we were out on the platform, Colonel Steele tapped me on the shoulder. "Kip, that's why I never carry anything valuable in my briefcase. It's the first thing they steal." He opened a button on his shirt to show me a slim leather pouch with a wax seal tucked inside his belt. He smiled.

---

2.   Editor's Note: An interesting expression, which may shed light on the origins of some of Robert Service's poetry. Service also described Black Moran's voice as "bedrock grit," but didn't arrive in the Yukon until 1904 when he worked at the bank in Whitehorse. Perhaps the bank manager told the Black Moran story to Robert Service too.

"Black Moran's gang just stole my toothbrush and a stale ham and cheese sandwich!"

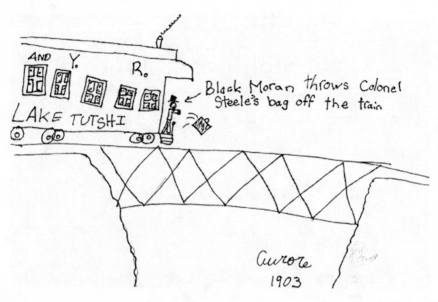

Above: Black Moran throwing Colonel Steele's briefcase into Dead Horse Gulch. Sketch by Aurore from Kip's scrapbook.

Chapter 6

Thurston Vanderbilt III

═══════════════════════════════════

"Alaska Border Bickering: Canadians Send 80 Page Long Argument to London"

—*The Skagway News*
June 24, 1903

We got off the train in Skagway and Colonel Steele went with the conductor to report the robbery. Percy was "in a state" as my teacher would say. I don't think Colonel Steele remembered to tell him that the secret documents were safe.

I wanted to go with Colonel Steele but Maman told me to carry the suitcases.

My sister Aurore made fun of me. "Thanks to your job at the White Horse Hotel, you must be *really* good at carrying suitcases. Here's mine!" She held out her suitcase and batted her eyelashes at me like a princess.

Sisters are like that. I picked up Papillon's suitcase but not Aurore's. Papillon's only had her stuffed bear, a book and—to my surprise and annoyance—a lot of rocks she had collected at Bennett. She wants to be a geologist when she grows up and is always looking for the mother lode[1], which is the place they say all the gold in the Yukon comes from.

Anyway, I dragged our suitcases to the Golden North Hotel. We were in Room 22, Colonel Steele was in Room 24 and Percy was

- 44 -

between us in Room 23. They tried to put us in Room 23, but everyone in Skagway knows that Room 23 at the Golden North is haunted by a girl named Mary who died there![2]

Above: Broadway Avenue in Skagway, Alaska, around the time of Kip's visit. Kip doesn't mention seeing Skagway's unique dog-drawn carriage. (Photo courtesy of MacBride Museum 1989-9-112)

---

1. Editor's note: Most of the gold in the Yukon is placer gold, which means it is loose and has settled in the bottoms of creek and rivers. There is a myth that somewhere in the mountains is a vast gold deposit that all these small flakes of placer gold have come from. No one has ever found it.
2. Editor's note: This is the earliest mention of the famous Golden North ghost. Even today she is rumoured to haunt room 23. Guests report seeing a strange shape in the room, sometimes after waking up unable to breathe. Some say the ghost is "Mary," a young woman who died of pneumonia in the room while waiting for her fiancé to return from a mining expedition.

Well, except Percy I guess. He was still fretting over the briefcase and seemed quite nervous.

While Maman was signing the hotel guest register, the door burst open and a crowd of people came in laughing loudly. It was Captain von Neidling with two men and a young woman. The strangers were obviously from Outside. In fact, they looked like they were extremely rich. One of the young men seemed to be the leader. He had a fancy suit jacket, hat and pinstriped pants. He carried a walking stick. It wasn't a real Yukon walking stick but was just for show. It was thin, with beautiful wood and had a silver handle with a jewel on top. Ten minutes of hiking on the Chilkoot Trail would have turned it into kindling.

His friend was dressed the same. I could see Aurore and Papillon staring at the woman's dress. It could have been out of an illustrated magazine from London.

"Well, Thurston, I think you'll find this hotel ... amusing!" joked Captain von Neidling. I had never seen him smile and joke.

"Well it's certainly not the Waldorf in New York," laughed Thurston. He flicked some dust off one of the tables with his gloves. "But it's all worth it if that mine of yours has as much gold as you say. I bought those shares for a reason!"

The woman pointed at the moose antlers on the wall and tittered. I could tell they were the kind of visitors who think Northern people are quaint and a bit slow.

Meanwhile, Aurore elbowed me in the ribs. Percy's face had turned from to twitchy to white. It looked like he was going to faint. He stared in amazement at the strangers.

"That's Sir Michael's wife's cousin!" Percy gasped as if everyone in the world would know what he was talking about and why it was important.

He pulled himself together and stretched out his hand. "Mr. Vanderbilt! Miss Vanderbilt![3] What an unexpected delight!" he said. I don't quite know how to describe how he said it. Aurore said that he "gushed." He acted like they were the most important people in the whole world. Colonel Steele told us later that his name was Thurston Vanderbilt III. The 'III' means that he was the third in his family to have the same name after his father and grandfather. I guess it's something rich people in New York do to help them keep track of who has all the money.

Thurston was a cousin or something to Percy's boss, Ambassador Sir Michael Herbert in Washingon. I remember the name since Percy always talked about the ambassador like he was a kind of god.

Anyway, Captain von Neidling finally noticed Percy and us. The look on his face reminded me of Mrs. Flanagan when she had Maman over one Sunday afternoon for a fancy tea party and Yves carried a dead gopher in through the front door.

We went upstairs to our room. "The ghost is in there. I can feel it," said Papillon confidently as we walked past Room 23. "But don't worry, Mary is a friendly ghost." I wasn't so sure about this since I'd heard stories about people waking up choking. I don't really believe in ghosts. I couldn't feel anything. But Papillon sometimes startles the family with things like that.

Aurore seemed to be thinking the same thing. "Should we tell Percy?" she said with a mischievous smirk.

A few minutes later, Percy knocked on our door. The old Percy who treated us like country bumpkins was gone. Now he needed our help.

"I have to get on the ship to Vancouver tomorrow. But with Thurston Vanderbilt here …" He seemed puzzled as to what to do. "I know! We'll get Y1 to follow them."

"Y1?" I said. I remembered that I wasn't supposed to know about Y1. After all, the only way we knew about it was because Papillon

3.   Editor's note: Sir Michael Herbert was British Ambassador to the United States at the time. His wife was American and was related to two of the richest families in the world: the Vanderbilts and the Astors. Presumably Thurston Vanderbilt III was one of these relations, although there is no evidence in the archives to substantiate his role in this story.

had been hanging upside down in a tree when Colonel Steele and Percy talked about it in our backyard!

"Yes! Yes! No one is to know! You'll be Y1's messenger. But ... damn! There's no time to meet Y1 and explain our code to him or how he should send us messages!"

I was surprised. What was going on? I was pretty sure Y1 didn't exist. Or, actually, that Colonel Steele was telling Percy that everything we told him was actually coming from an imaginary adult agent named Y1 since Percy would never believe anything a kid said.

This gave me an idea. "You could show Aurore and me," I said. "We'll explain it to Y1." Percy didn't like this very much, but he didn't have much choice.

He got out a pad of paper and a pencil. He sighed like he was tired of explaining simple things to brainless colonials all the time. Then he took our copy of *Kim* out of Aurore's bag and ripped a piece of paper off the top of the pad and placed it right on the wooden desk. "Never write on the pad. It leaves marks on the paper underneath." Then he explained how to do a coded message.

It was hard to understand at first, but once we saw how it worked it was very easy. I'll explain how to do it at the end of the chapter.

After we had learned how to do it, he said one final thing: "Now this is very important! Tell Y1 that my code name will be Piccadilly. Never use my real name. And tell Y1 that when his message is encoded, he must burn the original copy. If someone finds it in his dustbin, they might match it with a copy of the telegram stolen from the telegraph office. Then they'll learn how to uncode all the messages! That might put Y1 in danger!"

I repeated what Percy had said to make sure I understood. Then Aurore did too.

Percy sighed. "We'll just have to hope for the best," he said.

A sudden thought occurred to me. "What is Colonel Steele's code name?"

"How about 'Bull Moose?'" suggested Aurore.

Percy just muttered something about colonials and went to his own room.

We went to bed. We heard Colonel Steele tromp up the hallway and enter his room. About ten minutes later, we heard him tromp back down the stairs. "It's 'Bull Moose.' Where's he going?" I asked Aurore.

"Silence!" said Maman. As you've probably guessed, that means "silence" in English.

How to Use a Book Code
by Kip Dutoit

Here's how to use a book code. It seems complicated at first, but it's easy once you figure it out. If you want to learn the details later, you can skip to the next chapter.

First you write your message out on a piece of paper and leave two blank lines under each line. Then you open your book at random and pick a page and line. Let's say page 23, line 7. Remember these numbers, since you'll start your message with "237" so your friend receiving the message knows which part of his or her book to use to decode the message. In fact, you'll write it twice: "237237." That's in case the telegraph operator makes a mistake, which happens a lot with telegrams.

Then you write the words from page 23, line 7 underneath your original message. Make sure you line up the letters so the first letter of line 7 is under the first letter of your message and so on.

Then you take each letter from your message, one at a time, and add it to the corresponding letter underneath it.

Say you want to send a secret message saying "The Golden North is haunted" and page 23, line 7 of your book says "Kim knew India like the back of his hand." Notice how the words from page 23 are broken up to line up under the words of your secret message (see example on next page).

Look at the letter "G" in "Golden." It's right above the letter "K" in "knew." In the alphabet "G" is letter number 7 and "K" is letter 11. Add them together and you get 18, which is letter "R" in the alphabet. So you put an "R" down on the third line as your coded message letter. This is the letter that you will send you your friend by telegram.

If your numbers add up to more than 26, then just subtract 26. Look at the first letter where "T" plus "K" equals 31. You just subtract 26. So 31 minus 26 is 5. So the coded letter there is "E," the fifth letter in the alphabet.

Original message:	The	Golden	North	is	haunted!
Page 23, line 7 (divided): Kim		knewln	diali	ke	theback
Coded message:	eqr	rcqanb	rcsfq	tx	bizpuho

After adding in the "237237" to tell your friend what part of the book to use, your telegram would read "237237 EQR RCQANB RCSFQ TX BIZPUHO!" There's an extra part Percy didn't tell us about, but Colonel Steele told me that for extra security you divide up everything into groups of five letters. That way no one can guess that a two letter word like "TX" above is likely to be "is" or "to" or something like that. If you did that, your message would read "23723 7EQRR CQANB RCSFQ TZBIZ UHO!"

To uncode something, you just do it backwards. Try it out for yourself. Decode the message on the telegram below using this sentence: "Yukon blueberries are the best." Remember that if you get a negative number, it means the numbers added up to more than 26 when being coded and your friend subtracted 26. That means you need to add 26 back now.

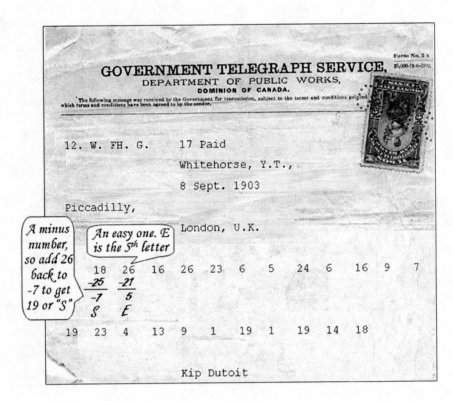

Above: Example of Kip's book code.

Chapter 7

The Ghost of the Golden North

"U.S. Senators Tell President Not to Give Away Chilkoot Pass"

—Newspaper clipping from Mr. Taylor
June 24, 1903

"Aieeeeeee!"

We were woken by a scream. Aurore said it was "bloodcurdling." That means it makes your blood clump up inside you. Not really, but you know what I mean.

I wish I knew as many great words as Aurore. Maybe I should read while I fish.

Anyway, it was Percy next door. There were thrashing noises from his room. I thought I heard footsteps going down the stairs, but I wasn't sure. They were very light footsteps, not heavy ones like Colonel Steele's.

We ran out into the hallway. Percy was there in his nightshirt, which looked exactly what you would expect a fancy fellow from London to sleep in. He even had a night cap! "I thought I saw a woman in my room! Standing at the foot of the bed!" He shuddered. "She looked like a ghost!"

"Can you breathe all right?" asked Papillon. Percy nodded. "Told you!" she said to us. "Mary's not a mean ghost. I think people just made up those stories about the ghost choking people in Room 23."

Percy's eyes bulged. He glanced at the "23" on his door. "I say!" he gasped.

Papillon ignored him. "I wonder why she wanted to wake you up just now!"

Just then, I definitely heard footsteps on the stairs. Colonel Steele bounded around the corner.

"Just an ... err ... nightmare, Colonel Steele," said Percy. "Nothing to worry about."

"He says he saw a ghost," said Yves.

"Nothing of the kind!" sputtered Percy. He looked embarrassed.

"He saw Mary?" said Colonel Steele to Papillon. She nodded. "Hmmm ..." said Colonel Steele. I don't think he believes in ghosts. But he seemed puzzled.

Suddenly, he froze. He crouched down and picked up two tiny pieces of acorn—spruce cone to be exact—that lay on the floor by his door. "Somebody's been in my room," he whispered. He swung the door open and flicked on the light. It was empty. We followed him in, but he signalled us to wait by the door. He moved to his desk, where some papers and books were visible. He looked carefully at the books from several angles.

"Yup. Someone's been here. Maybe they heard Percy's caterwauling and fled."

"I was not caterwauling, Steele!" complained Percy, but Colonel Steele didn't even look at him. Instead, he kept looking at his books from various angles.

"Percy, does caterwauling mean crying really loud like a baby so they can hear you through the walls?" asked Yves.

"Yes," replied Percy. "I mean, yes, but ... oh, never mind!" He pursed his lips and looked at us in annoyance.

"Colonel Steele, how do you know someone was here?" I asked.

"I always leave the top book of the pile so its bottom edge points at the corner of the desk." We leaned over and looked. Colonel Steele put his walking stick along the bottom edge of the top book on the pile. The stick pointed off the side of the table. Then he moved it so that the stick was over the corner of the desk. "That's how I left it earlier today," he said.

"That way you know when someone has been moving your books around!" said Aurore.

Colonel Steele pulled a small sprig of spruce tree out of his pocket. "And you close little pieces of spruce cone in the door, so that when someone opens it you know they've been in your room! Something I learned in South Africa," said Colonel Steele proudly. He showed us how to pull off a piece or two and wedge it in the door. "Except it's Africa so they have different trees there."

Maman was watching the whole time. "Monsieur le Colonel!" she barked suddenly. I think she realized what Colonel Steele was telling us. I recognized the look in her eye. She knew we were up to things that kids probably shouldn't be involved in.

"Oh right!" For once, Colonel Steele looked guilty. He stood up and looked sort of sheepish. "Adult stuff. Move along. Back to bed."

We trooped back to our room. As we passed Percy's door Papillon said, "Don't worry. Mary won't hurt you." Percy didn't look reassured.

As you can guess, it took a long time for us to get back to sleep. Maman had to say "silence" about a hundred times. I couldn't help thinking about all the questions. Did the burglars get Colonel Steele's secret papers this time? Was it Black Moran or someone else? Maybe even Captain von Neidling? Why was Percy so worried about getting messages to Y1? What did Thurston Vanderbilt III have to do with it?

I was still thinking about these questions when I fell asleep.

We slept in the next day. When we woke up, Percy and Colonel Steele had already left to catch the early ship to Seattle. The Colonel left a note. "Kids, listen to you mother. Go home and study hard at school. Don't worry. I've still got the <u>package</u>." He underlined the word package, so he must have meant the secret documents.

"I wish we'd been able to say goodbye to Colonel Steele before he left," I said. "Too bad his boat left so early. I'd like to ask him who he thinks burgled his room."

Above: Yukon River life in Kip's day. Bill Taylor of Taylor & Drury loading firewood on a riverboat similar to one owned by Kip's father. The photo was found in Kip's scrapbook but must be from after Kip's story since Bill appears here as an adult. (Photo courtesy of the Bill & Aline Taylor collection)

"And why they burgled it," said Aurore. "And I guess we should have told him about Percy asking us to pass messages to Y1."

"Well," I said. "I don't think we'll hear from Percy again. I just wish I knew how it all turned out."

I thought about that as I got dressed. Was it Black Moran again? But what did he have to do with secret documents about the Alaskan border? I could see him stealing money. But papers?

But I quickly forgot all this as we went through our Skagway "ritual."

Do you know what a ritual is? It's when you always do the same thing. Our family has a ritual we do every time we visit Skagway. First we have a fancy breakfast. I always order the same thing: a huge pile of sourdough pancakes with blueberry syrup. Then we walk down to the water, where we play on the beach and watch the seals and eagles. D'Artagnan usually gets completely soaked. Then we walk up Broadway and visit Tina's store on our way to pay our respects to Frank Reid in the cemetery. Tina helped Aurore and Yves when they were stuck in Skagway with Soapy Smith, so we always stop and say hello.

Maman was very keen on our ritual the morning that Colonel Steele and Percy left. I think she was trying to get us back to normal after all the excitement. She likes Colonel Steele, but I don't think she considers him "normal."

First we went to Mrs. Robinson's restaurant on Broadway. She is always happy to see us. She is one of those people who can't stop themselves from saying "How you've grown!" and messing up your hair. "Tousling your hair," is what she calls it. I think it means doing something to bother boys. Yves usually hides behind Maman's skirt, but Mrs. Robinson always tousles him in the end.

She always brings me an extra pancake. That's pretty nice, since each pancake is the size of a plate! When she brings the plates she always stops to talk to us and tell us things like where she picked the blueberries. That's nice, of course, but Maman will never let me start eating until Mrs. Robinson is done talking. You have to sit there politely holding your fork and knife, with the steam rising out of your pancakes and the butter slowly melting off the side (taking a blueberry or two with it) as Aurore translates Maman and Mrs. Robinson talking about making blueberry jelly. It's like torture!

Anyway, my brother and sisters like Mrs. Robinson too. She always puts whip cream in the shape of a happy face on Yves's and Papillon's pancakes. And she calls Aurore "Mademoiselle."

"That's nothing special," I pointed out. "It just means 'miss' in French."

Aurore was offended. "It's very fancy if you say it in English," she claimed. She cut her pancake carefully just like the Queen does it, with her knife in her right hand and her fork in the left. She put a small piece in her mouth. Then she patted her lips with her napkin. Only barbarians rub their napkins across their mouths like they are cleaning a window, she keeps telling me.

I noticed Maman was looking at my fork, which had an entire pancake hanging from it. Her eyebrows arched.

"Cram it in all in at once! Like a miner!" encouraged Yves mischievously. My pancake hung over my plate dripping syrup. Maman's eyebrows went higher.

I put my pancake back on my plate and cut a smaller piece.

Yves waited until Maman was talking to Papillon. "Kip, try that piece of bacon," he whispered. "All at once!"

Chapter 8

Teddy Bear

"Canadian Delegation Gets Ready to Leave for London"

—Newspaper clipping from Mr. Taylor
June 24, 1903

After breakfast, we continued our ritual. We untied D'Artagnan from in front of the restaurant. Then we threw rocks in the ocean and watched the seals play in the sun. After that, we walked up Broadway and said hello to Tina in her shop. Then we walked out to the cemetery to put flowers on Frank Reid's grave. Aurore began to cry. She always does when we visit the cemetery. I never tease her about it. She was friends with Mr. Reid. He tried to help Maman after Soapy Smith stole all her money during the Gold Rush.

Yves was crying too. "Why do the good people have to die?" he asked. Maman didn't seem to have an answer for that one.

We stopped and looked at Soapy's grave too. It was just outside the cemetery fence. People didn't think a bad guy should be buried inside a proper cemetery. But the grass was trampled all around Soapy's grave as if lots of people had visited it. It's funny how people seem more interested in the bad guy than the good guy.

On the way back to town, we walked past some people standing around a dog sled in someone's backyard. They looked so different from regular people in Skagway you couldn't help noticing them.

There was a man in a big city suit. Not as fancy as Thurston Vander-bilt III's, but nicer than usual in Alaska. He reminded me of a professor. He was telling the others about the dog sled.

Then there was a lady, a giant man with hands the size of a grizzly bear's paws, and another man in a long coat. He had a hat pulled down low over his head.

"The man in the coat is the boss," said Yves. Once he said it, I realized he was right. The way they were standing was a clue. But the main thing was that the professor was speaking only to the man with his face hidden by the hat. It was as if he had forgotten the others were there.

As we walked past, we couldn't help stopping to listen.

"This is a typical Alaskan dog sleigh. We've got one just like it at the Smithsonian," the professor said. Aurore looked sideways at me. We would never call a dog sled a "sleigh." Santa drives a sleigh.

"What's the Smithsonian?" I whispered.

"The big museum in Washington, D.C.," she whispered back. She gave me a sisterly look as if it was the sort of thing you were supposed to know. She's been like that ever since she started reading the encyclopaedia from A to Z. It was pretty annoying at first. All we could talk about at dinner were aardvarks, antelopes and Argentina. But now that she's made it past "S" it might come in handy.

Meanwhile, the professor seemed to have noticed that we were listening. He cleared his throat. "Hrumff ... Yes, a typical dog sleigh. A very common Alaskan mode of transportation. The driver attaches 8–12 dogs to it in a fan shape-"

"That's not right!" piped up Yves.

The professor stopped. Then he tried to continue, ignoring Yves. "err ... a fan shape, using a whip to drive the Saint Bernards or similar dogs—"

"Huskies!" said Yves. "Malamutes!" said Papillon.

I could see the lady and the man in the hat looking at us. The professor tried to ignore us again. "As I was saying, err, there are reports that some Alaskans have succeeded in using mooses to pull their sleighs—"

Above: Theodore Roosevelt in his Rough Riders uniform in 1898 during the Spanish-American War. He was President of the United States five years later during the Alaska-Canada border dispute. (Photo courtesy of the Library of Congress).

"Hey!" we all shouted.

"That's not right either!" I said.

Yves was indignant. "Mister, every two-year-old knows you don't say 'mooses!'"

"Excuse me," said the professor in annoyance. He spoke slowly and in that tone adults use with stupid children. "Now children, please don't bother the adults—"

But before he could finish, the man in the hat cut him off. "What do you mean it's not right?" he asked. He was looking at me.

I'll never forget his eyes when he asked me that question. They seemed to cut into me like a giant mining drill. All his energy seemed to come straight through his thick glasses and right at me. He wasn't asking just to be polite. It was as if, at that moment, finding out how to set up an Alaskan dog sled was the most important thing in the world to him.

For a moment I was speechless as I stared back at those giant energetic eyes.

The professor spoke first. "Let's get back to the sleigh, Mr. President—"

"You're supposed to call me Mr. Smith," growled the man, never taking his eyes off me. "Now, young fellow, tell me what you mean."

It took me a second. I knew all about sleds. But it was hard to get the words out. I stuttered for a second and then started. "Well, you never attach dogs to the sled in a fan shape," I said. "You do it in pairs in a straight line. Your lead dog up front and your wheel dogs at the back."

The professor butted in again. "The fan is well documented. We have photographic evidence at the Smithsonian," he finished, as if whatever the Smithsonian thought had to be true. The man glanced at the professor then back at me. I could tell he was enjoying himself. He was waiting to see if I could win an argument with the professor.

I looked at the professor. "How could you get a fan of dogs up the Dawson Trail?" I asked. "It's only three feet wide between the trees in some places. The dogs would get hopelessly tangled!" I held out my arms to show how wide three feet was.

The professor's mouth dropped open a little bit. The man looked at the professor. There was a twinkle in his eye as he watched the professor try to think of something to say.

"And you hardly ever have to whip huskies. They love to run and pull."

"What about the moose?" asked the man in the hat.

"You'd never get one near a sled. They're dangerous!" I replied.

"But good eating?"

"You bet!"

The man in the hat waved us all over. Pretty soon we were sitting on the grass telling him all kinds of things about the North. He was a very curious man. He just kept asking us questions. He didn't pretend to know everything already. If he didn't know something, he'd ask. He didn't mind if people thought he might look dumb.

He asked us about the Chilkoot Pass, the Yukon River, the train and all kinds of things. He was very interested in the plants and animals, especially birds. It turned out he had published a book on birds, but he had never heard how we call the Grey Jay a "camprobber" or "whiskeyjack."

He even pulled out a notebook and wrote down some of our answers. He didn't seem to know how to spell, since he wrote things like "Alaskan bers eet sammun" and "dog sled not dog slay." He wrote down all the Northern words he heard. He loved "cheechako" and "sourdough" the most.

The lady was very curious too. When she found out Maman didn't speak English, she started asking Aurore and Papillon all kinds of questions. You know, how they kept the house warm, what kind of food they cooked, what kind of clothes they wore in the winter when they were skiing or skating. She seemed surprised. I guess Yukon girls did a lot more than girls in Washington.

"You mean you chop the wood?" she asked Aurore in amazement.

"Yes ma'am. But just the kindling. I'm not big enough to lift the big logs."

"And you know how to shoot a gun?"

"No, ma'am. But my Dad says he'll teach me when I'm twelve. Then we can go grouse hunting together."

This amused the man in the hat. "Edith, I told you that I needed to get you a gun!" He slapped me on the back, something he appeared to like doing. "Son, the Northland must be just about the best place for a kid to grow up. Freedom! Adventure! Self-reliance! You know, the strenuous life!"

Finally, the lady turned to my mother. "Madame, I just realized how rude we've been. We haven't introduced ourselves. I'm Edith Roosevelt and this is my husband Theodore.[1]" My sisters and Maman curtsied. Yves and I shook President Roosevelt's hand.

I think the president was already bored of the professor, and he'd taken a liking to us for some reason, so much to our surprise he invited us for dinner.

"Yes!" we all cried.

"Non," replied Maman. "Juste parce qu'il est le Président des Etats-Unis ne veut pas dire qu'il est un hôte approprié pour les enfants impressionnables."

"I'm not impressionable," said Yves.

---

1.   Editor's note: This is just one of the amazing revelations in Kip's report. Previously, historians had believed that President Roosevelt never visited Alaska. He was certainly an avid hunter and outdoorsman. As Captain Richardson notes in Chapter 3, it became increasingly difficult to escape the newspapers once he became President. He must have hoped that a secret trip to Alaska would allow him the freedom to hunt, fish and camp like he had previously. He seems to have succeeded, since his trip remained secret until Kip's story was unearthed.

"Come on! Of course President Roosevelt is an appropriate host for kids," I pleaded in French.

But Maman wasn't convinced. I think she remembered that time we met a Member of Parliament outside the Malamute Saloon.

Fortunately, I think Mrs. Roosevelt understood Maman's worry. Aurore translated for Mrs. Roosevelt as she assured Maman there would be no smoking, card playing or shooting. All three seemed to cause some disappointment to President Roosevelt, but he was so keen to hear how grizzlies caught salmon and miners found gold that I guess he didn't mind.

Chapter 9

Dinner with President Roosevelt

"I wish I had more twelve-year-old boys in my Cabinet!"

—*President Theodore Roosevelt, in my journal*
June 24, 1903

We were very excited when Maman finally agreed that President and Mrs. Roosevelt were "proper" and that we could have dinner with them. They were staying at a lodge on the edge of town. As we walked there, the president kept asking me questions about the Yukon and stopping to write down the answers.

He saw my curiosity. "Don't wonder, Kip! Ask!"

"Why do you write everything down?" I asked.

"Helps me remember. I can never remember a name if you tell me it. But if I write it down, it's there forever."

"Why do you spell everything wrong? Like S-A-M-M-U-N instead of S-A-L-M-O-N?"

"Kip, you're sounding like the professor already! What do you mean wrong? It's different, yes, but I say it's better. Every word is spelled like it sounds. What do you think of that?"

I thought about Mr. Galpin's English class. "It's a great idea, Mr. President. Everybody should do it."

"I agree. But the experts don't." He glanced behind and whispered. "The professor hates the idea. They'd have to redo every label at the Smithsonian! Besides, everyone is so used to the old system. If one person started writing that way, everyone else would think he was crazy."

"But you're the president!" I said. "Isn't it your job to get everybody to do something when it's good for the whole country?" President Roosevelt stopped. He thought for a moment, then laughed and slapped my back. "I wish I had more twelve-year-old boys in my Cabinet," he said to his wife.

"A twelve-year-old president is probably enough," she said.[1]

As we walked, I was surprised to hear the president start talking about when he was a kid. You would never guess that he had asthma as a boy and that the other kids made fun of him!

He told me he thought I was the luckiest boy in the world to grow up in a place like the Yukon. "Think about it Kip! The freedom! The adventure! The challenges! The outdoor life is so much more uplifting than living in a city. You learn to just do what needs to be done and not to worry about the doubters and naysayers. Why, I bet you've had more scrapes and adventures already than most twenty-year-old men in Boston!" That made me think. I'd been feeling pretty sorry for myself with my Dad in the hospital and Rudi making fun of me all the time.

But before I could say anything, President Roosevelt was already onto the next topic. Talking to him was like that! He started telling me about the Yosemite Valley. You pronounce it "Yo-sem-i-tee." He

---

1. Editor's Note: Kip is probably lucky that his role in President Roosevelt's widely mocked attempts to reform English spelling have not come to light before now. In 1906 the President ordered the U.S. Government printer to adopt simplified spelling, which resulted in his famous Thanksgiving Address: "When nerly three centuries ago, the first settlers kam to the kuntry which has bekom this great republik, tha confronted not only hardship and privashun, but terible risk of thar lives…. The kustum has now bekum nashnul and hallowed by immemorial usaj." To the dismay of schoolchildren the effort was widely ridiculed. Roosevelt thought the word "thru" was the most controversial. He was forced to abandon the system shortly afterwards.

said he'd just been on a big camping trip there and that it was the most beautiful place he'd ever been before Alaska.

"They're making a hash of it though, Kip! Yosemite should be a national treasure. But before you know it, the trees will be gone and there'll be a railroad right across it!"

"Why don't you fix it?"

"Oh,' he sighed. "It's State of California land. Plus, I don't think the Congress would pay for it!"

I looked at him. "What?" he said. Then he laughed. "I see! You want me to take my own medicine. Never mind the doubters and naysayers!" He pulled his notebook out of his pocket, opened it to a page that had "To Do: NOW!!!" written on it and made a note.[2]

Their lodge was very nice. I had no idea that rich people came to Alaska just to visit and pretend to live in a cabin. There was a great big fireplace and living room, plus a cook. Everyone called him the "chef." That's another French word that is extra fancy if you say it in English.

To my surprise, the rich New York people from our hotel were coming for dinner too. Thurston Vanderbilt III was standing by the fire warming his feet and drinking a fancy drink with a little paper umbrella in it. "A bunch of cheechakos," whispered the president to me. "But I've got to be nice to them. Half the blowhards in the Senate are Thurston's uncles! Even worse, the rest of the family owns newspapers!"

The big, burly man who we had met earlier now turned out to be the president's body guard. He was nice. He brought us warm milk and cookies. You could barely see the glass inside his enormous hands.

---

2.   Editor's Note: In May 1903, Roosevent spent four days in Yosemite with Sierra Club founder John Muir. At some point over the summer of 1903 he made a decision to further protect the Yosemite valley. Three years later, Roosevelt signed a law to bring Yosemite under federal control and preserve it for the nation.

We couldn't figure out what was going on with the hot milk and everybody warming their hands by the fire. It was the middle of summer! But they were all complaining about the cold. I guess it gets pretty hot in Washington, D.C.

Thurston must have been really rich. Or just bad mannered. Anyway, he seemed to like teasing the president. "Mr. President, we were just out hunting with that Neidling fellow. Apparently everyone in Alaska thinks you're just bluffing about the border. They're just waiting for you to cave in to the British and the softies in Washington and give away the shop!"

The president wasn't amused. In fact, his answer was sort of a growl. "He can think what he wants. It's not a bluff."

Thurston laughed. "Well, I hope you mean what you say, Mr. President."

"I always say what I mean and mean what I say. Tell him to read my book about our last war with the British. With a navy like ours, we shouldn't be scared of any country on earth."[3]

"Glad to hear it! My shares in Star Mine won't be worth yesterday's newspaper if it turns out to be on Canadian land!"

The president sort of sighed. "That's what your uncle in the Senate keeps telling me too." The president pretended to tie his boot and whispered in my ear. "People like that are the hardest part about being president."

At dinner, the president wanted to talk about Alaskan mountains. You really have no idea what President Roosevelt is going to say next. This time, it turned out that he was the leader of only the third expedition to ever get to the top of Mont Blanc, a really famous mountain in Europe. The president clearly wanted to be the first person to the top of Mount McKinley in Alaska. It's the highest mountain

---

3. Editor's Note: *The Naval War of 1812*, written by Roosevelt when he was just 23. It became the standard history of the conflict for a generation and is still in print.

in North America. He kept asking if anyone had heard whether Judge Wickersham had made it or not.[4]

Thurston told us all about their day. "Charming fellow, that Nei-dling. Got us a local guide. We shot a bear!" he said proudly.

"Where?" exclaimed the president.

Thurston and his sister spoke at the same time. "The forest!" said Thurston. "The dump!" said the sister. Aurore's eyebrows edged upwards. So did President Roosevelt's. I don't think either approved of hunting at the dump.

But Thurston carried on. "And then we chopped down some trees. Was that ever fun."

The sister interrupted again. "Some boring men complained that one of the trees fell on the Chilkoot Trail, but I just told them that Alaska was full of trees that fall all over the place and that they should learn to live with it if they haven't already!" Thurston and she seemed to think this was very funny.

"We also picked up the greatest souvenir. It's a sign off an aban-doned tavern called the 'Last Chance Saloon.' It'll look great over the bar at the guest house at the Hamptons."[5]

Aurore glanced at me. Was it all right to take stuff from the Chilk-oot Trail back to New York just because you thought it would be a fun souvenir?

The president seemed puzzled too. "Why were you cutting down trees?" he asked.

"To see them fall. They make such a huge racket when they smash into the other trees!"

---

4.   Editor's Note: The Wickersham expedition did not make it to the summit of Mount McKinley in 1903. The mountain would remain unclimbed until 1913, when an Alaskan aboriginal man named Walter Harper reached the summit as part of the Stuck Expedition.

5.   Editor's Note: There is no record of a "Last Chance Saloon" on the early stages of the Chilkoot Trail, perhaps because Thurston Vanderbilt III shipped the sign to New York.

Suddenly, Papillon spoke up. All you could see was her head sticking up above her plate. And her stuffed bear. Maman normally didn't allow stuffed animals at the table, but Papillon seemed to think this was a special occasion. "There are too many people chopping down trees and shooting bears. Pretty soon there won't be any left." Thurston and his sister stared at Papillon in amazement. Papillon turned to President Roosevelt. "Wasting trees is bad, isn't it Mr. President?"

The president laughed. "Exactly right, mademoiselle. I think I'll pass a law to that effect."

"Thank you. That's very nice," said Papillon. "If you do I'll rename my bear 'Theodore' in your honour ... or maybe 'Teddy' since that sounds better."[6]

---

6.   Editor's Note: This incident is the first recorded episode of President Roosevelt considering forest protection. One must wonder if he got the idea for his 1905 creation of the U.S. Forest Service during his visit to Alaska, perhaps from Papillon Dutoit. Also, in 1906 he signed the Antiquities Act to prevent the looting of historic sites, although it is not clear if this would have protected recent sites such as the Chilkoot Trail. Papillon's renaming of her bear is just one of many possible origins of the phrase Teddy Bear, all of which are associated with Theodore Roosevelt. One of the most famous involves Roosevelt refusing to shoot a captured bear, calling it "unsportsmanlike" and releasing the animal.

Chapter 10

TR Rides Again

"I'm not bluffing. I sent the U.S. Army to Alaska for a reason. I won't be the president who loses the Alaska Panhandle!"

—*President Roosevelt, in my journal*
June 24, 1903

We hated leaving President Roosevelt and Mrs. Roosevelt after dinner. The president was just beginning to tell us all his stories about the Rough Riders at the Battle of San Juan Hill in Cuba, his time as a cowboy in North Dakota and his adventures in Colorado. Did you know that he once arrested three men when he was a deputy sheriff? Or that he won a medal for leading the charge up San Juan Hill, and then lost it when he complained too loudly to the General after the battle that his men weren't getting proper hospital care?[1] You could tell he was enjoying telling his stories again, and he was just as disappointed as we were when Maman made us go home at 8 o'clock for bed.

---

1. Editor's Note: Kip is referring to the Battle of San Juan Hill, one of the most famous battles in the Spanish-American War in 1898. Roosevelt was Lieutenant Colonel of a volunteer cavalry regiment named the Rough Riders. At the critical moment, with no orders from his commanding officer, Roosevelt took the initiative and charged his troops up the hill. Fighting was bloody but the Rough Riders captured the hill. Roosevelt became a national hero.

I begged to stay later. "But Maman! Other parents would let their kids stay up late with the president of the United States!"

"Another half an hour won't hurt them, ma'am!" said the president, joining in.

"Theodore!" said Mrs. Roosevelt sharply. "Wait until you've raised your six children perfectly before interfering with someone else's kids." The president shifted in his seat.[2] Believe it or not, he looked like a kid who's been caught trying to steal an extra cookie from the jar.

Maman was still looking at me sharply. Her eyebrow twitched upwards.

"Looks like we're beat, Kip," said the president, slapping me on the shoulder.

"I know, Maman," I said dejectedly. "Just because other parents allow it doesn't mean it's right." It was one of Maman's favourite sayings.

We said our goodbyes and moped home in the drizzle. Except for Yves. He galloped ahead. Instead of pretending to be one of the Three Musketeers, like he usually did, tonight he was one of Teddy Roosevelt's Rough Riders. The glow of the Midnight Sun came through the thick clouds and we could see Yves down the street as he waved a stick for a sword and shouted "charge."

Our dog D'Artagnan was very happy to see us back at the hotel. He'd been tied up all evening. Maman agreed to let us take him for a short walk before bed.

D'Artagnan was full of energy that night. The rain had finally stopped and Alaska seemed to be alive with smells and night time noises. He bounded up Broadway through the puddles, then smelled a squirrel or something and raced into an alley. We chased after him through the puddles too. We were probably already in

---

2.   Editor's Note: The Roosevelt children were controversial at the White House. Referring to his daughter Alice, Roosevelt once said: "I can be President of the United States, or I can control Alice. I cannot possibly do both."

trouble for getting our shoes wet. If we lost the dog and were late, Maman would kill us.

We found D'Artagnan standing at the bottom of a tree sniffing around. It was a big old cottonwood with a forest of willows beside it. I saw a cat jump off the tree on to a roof and scurry away. It was a black cat, but with a flash of white on its tail. Did that mean good luck or bad luck? Don't be silly, I told myself. You don't need good luck if you're just walking the dog.

I was just about to call to D'Artagnan when I heard a door slam down Broadway and footsteps hurry towards us.

Something told me we should be quiet. "Shhh ..." I whispered to Yves. I pulled him back into the shadows behind the willow. Yves put his arms around D'Artagnan's neck. Our dog knew he should be quiet too.

A large, cold drop of water fell off the branch above me and went right down my neck. Yves sniggered. I shushed him again.

The "clump clump" noise of boots on the boardwalk along Broadway changed suddenly to "scrunch scrunch" as the footsteps turned onto the gravel up our alley. The thick, black clouds made it seem much darker than the usual Midnight Sun summer night in Alaska.

We glimpsed two black shapes approaching. One was in the lead and the other had to hop ahead every few steps to keep up. The first one didn't seem to care his friend couldn't keep up.

They splashed noisily into the puddle right in front of us.

"Gumbo!" said one of the men. "This Alaska mud'll suck your boots right off!" He cursed and spat. It was Black Moran!

I bit my lip and pulled Yves further back into the shadows behind the tree. Black Moran spat again and looked up at the clouds. He had a big black bundle under one arm. He seemed to be in an even worse mood than normal. "Neidling's got a lot of nerve sending us out in the middle of a rainstorm for this!" he said angrily.

"What's it got in it?" said the other fellow with a wheeze. He was still puffing from trying to keep up with Black Moran.

"Nothing!" said Black Moran. "That's the point. I already looked. Nothing but Sam Steele's stupid razor and toothbrush, a book about Africa and another about some girl named Kim."

"Oh. That's a great story. Kim's actually a boy and—"

The water splashed as Black Morin turned suddenly to face the other fellow. "Shut up about the book!" he said viciously. He punched the other fellow in the shoulder. "I should have known you were a reader." He said it as if reading were some kind of terrible disease.

"Jeez! Lay off," said the other fellow, rubbing his arm. "The Bible's a book too."

Black Moran raised his arm as if to punch the man again.

I glanced nervously at D'Artagnan. He was tense and I was afraid he was going to bark at the men. Yves hugged him tighter.

"Look," said Black Moran savagely. He began to look for keys in his pockets. "We tore those books to pieces page by page and didn't find what Neidling was looking for. And since it was my idea to dump Steele's bag in the creek to dispose of the evidence, Neidling got the idea to make me go back to the creek and fish it out."

"At night in the middle of a rainstorm?"

"Yes," said Black Moran. "Now if that happened to a character in one of your books, how would he feel?"

"Angry?" asked the other man.

The sun glowed through the clouds for a moment and I saw Black Moran smile. "Exactly," he replied. Then he punched the other man hard in the arm again. "Let's drop this bag off inside and get back to the Red Onion." They unlocked the door and went inside. The light came on for a few minutes, then it went off again as the men reappeared at the door. They locked up and disappeared down the alley.

I looked sideways at Yves. He and D'Artagnan looked back at me.

Suddenly, a voice hissed into my ear from the fence just behind us. "Who were those men?" Yves and I jumped straight up into the air and D'Artagnan woofed in surprise.

Above: The Telegraph Office in Whitehorse where Kip worked. (Photo courtesy of MacBride Museum 1990-23-1-483)

It was President Roosevelt. You could tell he was delighted that he had been able to sneak up on us. "How do you think I bagged all those mountain lions in Colorado? By walking up to them in squeaky shoes?" He hopped over the fence. He was very nimble for a president.

I explained who Black Moran was and how he had just dropped off Sam Steele's stolen bag.

The president nodded. "Sam Steele. Met him in New York after I was Police Commissioner. Quite a fellow." I expected him to go on and say we should find the police. Instead, he glanced quickly over his shoulder and said, "What should we do now? Break into the building and get the bag back?"

"Well—" I stuttered. The thought had crossed my mind, but it didn't seem right coming out of the president's mouth.

"Yes!" said Yves enthusiastically. "The Rough Riders would do it for sure!"

"You bet!" whispered President Roosevelt with excitement. "One time in Cuba we snuck into the house where a Spanish colonel was living and stole all his papers. We found out exactly how many men and horses he had."

I realized suddenly that President Roosevelt was like the boy in your class who always comes up with the ideas that get you in trouble. He still thought like a twelve-year-old boy![3] Except he wasn't in school anymore, he was the president!

Something in the back of my head told me we really should go find a policeman, but Yves and the president were so keen I just told them my plan. "Good plan, Kip," said the president with a big smile. "You'd be a natural in the Rough Riders." His moustache twitched in anticipation.

Before we could start our plan, though, Yves interrupted with one of his questions that come out of nowhere. "Mr. President Roosevelt sir, would you really attack Canada with your army?"

The president looked down at him. He looked serious for a minute. "Well, Yves, I wouldn't want to. Our countries should be friends," he said. I could tell he was answering seriously. He never talked to us like we were just kids. "But I've got to stand up for my country and protect our border. If you read the old treaty, it's pretty clear Skagway belongs to America. The American people won't stand for giving up part of their country. So I'm not bluffing. I sent the U.S. Army to Alaska for a reason. I won't be the president who loses the Alaska Panhandle!"

I thought I heard him mutter, "Especially with an election next year." But Yves was already asking another question.

---

3. Editor's note: interestingly, a foreign ambassador in Washington once said exactly the same thing about President Roosevelt.

"What does bluffing mean, Mr. President Roosevelt, sir?" asked Yves.

"Yves, just call me TR," said the president. "And bluffing is when you say you're going to do something to get your way, but don't really mean it."

"Like when the mean boy in my class says he's going to beat me up if I don't give him my lunch, but I know he won't because he's really scared of my big brother Kip?"

"Exactly. The British are Canada's big brother, but I'm not scared of them. I'm not bluffing. That's exactly what I told the Germans a few months ago after their fleet bombarded Venezuela. Admiral Dewey and the U.S. Navy were ready. The Germans got the message."[4] He looked serious for a minute. "But boys, if there is a war, I want you and your family to stay home and be safe."

"Why is the border so important, TR? Is it because of the gold?" asked Yves.

The president laughed. "Well, let me tell you. Quite a few Senators own shares in Star Mine. It's right on the border and if it turns out to be loaded with gold, then it's as sure as shooting that there'll be a war! There wouldn't be a snowball's chance in Hawaii that America would let Canadian lawyers get a rich mine like that on our land!"

It looked like Yves and the president might talk about the border all night. The president opened his mouth as if he was going to say something else, but I had to interrupt. "Excuse me Mr. President, but Black Moran might be back any minute. We have to get going! Plus it's bedtime in 20 minutes and Maman will kill us if we're late!"

---

4.   Editor's Note: President Roosevelt is referring to the Venezuela Incident
      of 1902/03, mentioned by Colonel Steele earlier. As Roosevelt tells Kip,
      he let the Germans know that he would order Admiral Dewey's fleet to
      attack the German ships if they continued bombarding Venezuela.

Chapter 11

A Jump into the Dark

"Alaska Boundary Dispute: U.S. Sends 660 Pages to London to Make Its Case with Tribunal Judges!"

—Newspaper clipping from Mr. Taylor
June 25, 1903

"Right!" said the president. "Let's get going!"

We sent Yves and D'Artagnan down to the end of the alley to warn us if Black Moran came back. Then the president and I looked both ways down the alley and ran across to the door Black Moran had just locked. The lock looked brand new and solid.

The president pulled out a pocket knife and tried to fit it in the gap where the bolt was. I noticed that the handle was covered with jewels.

"Gift from the Emperor of Russia," he said when he noticed me staring. "A bit fancier than yours probably, but still solid." He fiddled for a few more minutes. "It's no use. I can't budge it." We stepped back and examined the wall. There was a window beside the door. This time, the Russian Emperor's knife did the trick. I heard a click as the latch moved, then the top part of the window popped open. It was pretty high and would be barely big enough for me to fit, but I could make it if I crawled in head first.

"Crawl in," said the president. "I'll hold your legs. Once you get in, you can unlock the door from the inside." He put his hands together

- 79 -

as a foothold for me. I stepped there, then on his shoulder and began to squirm in.

I was halfway through when I noticed all kinds of tools, shovels and other objects in the dark below. They cast black and dangerously pointy shadows as the glow from the Midnight Sun trickled in through the dirty window.

"Hold my legs! I'm in some kind of garage," I hissed at the president as I tried to scan the darkness to see where a safe landing spot might be.

Suddenly, I felt the president's grip on my leg tighten. I heard footsteps on the gravel. To my horror, they were coming from the other end of the alley. Not the end Yves and D'Artagnan were guarding.

"Theodore! What are you doing?" said a woman's voice loudly. She sounded like my Sunday School teacher when she catches me tying the laces of Aurore's boots together. I felt the president let go of my leg.

"Oh, err, hello Edith! Lovely night for a walk, isn't it?" he said with a stutter.

There was a long silence. I held on desperately with one hand on a workbench and my toes hooked into the window frame. Mrs. Roosevelt didn't seem very impressed.

"A walk?" she said. "Am I supposed to take you seriously, Theodore?"

"Well, umm, yes my love."

"What are you doing by that open window?" Another long pause. It seemed to last for minutes. The shovel shadows still jabbed dangerously up the walls. Suddenly, I noticed a strip of light coming from under another door at the back of the room. The words "Office" were barely visible in the dark. But before I could worry about *who* might be in the office, I heard Mrs. Roosevelt step closer.

"Theodore! Were you sneaking another cigar? You know what the doctor told you. Just one a day, after dinner!"

"You caught me, my love," sighed the president. Despite my predicament, I smiled to myself. I liked him more than ever. Better to get punished for smoking than trying to help a boy break into a criminal gang's garage! He really did think exactly like a twelve-year-old.

I heard their footsteps disappear down the alley. The president had left me, but I didn't mind. It was the Code of the Twelve-Year-Old Boy. If you're the only one who's been caught, take your punishment and don't give your pals away.

He knew I could just open the door from the inside and get out.

I held on for a few more seconds, then tried to let myself down onto the floor. I bit my lip as my pants got caught on a nail. I tried to pull carefully, but my arms were too tired. Suddenly I felt my pants rip and I collapsed. I was lucky. I fell mostly on the floor. I covered my head as some shovels, hockey sticks and other pointy objects fell onto me. "Quite a noise!" I said to myself. I was about to stand up and brush myself off when I heard a voice.

It was angry. It was loud. It was Captain von Neidling. "You heard me! Open the office door!" he barked. "There was just a noise in the garage."

I barely had a second to roll behind a garbage can when the office door opened and light flooded the room. I held perfectly still and hoped the can's shadow was big enough to hide my whole body.

"Don't see anything," said a voice. The inner door closed again. All I could hear was the beating of my heart and the blood pulsing in my ears. It seemed so loud that I wondered how Captain von Neidling couldn't hear it too.

I waited for my eyes to adjust to the darkness again. I stepped quietly towards the outer door. I didn't care about Colonel Steele's bag anymore. I just wanted to escape. I felt up the door and felt the cold metal of the new lock. My fingers felt all around it for a latch. But all I could find was the keyhole.

To my horror, I realized that it was the kind of lock that needs a key on the inside *and* outside. I must have taken a step backwards without realizing, since suddenly I heard another clang as something metal fell to the ground.

Captain von Neidling's voice barked again. "I told you! Go see what that is!"

Fortunately, my eyes were well adjusted to the darkness by then. I quickly saw there was nowhere to hide except right beside the office door. But that was actually closer to where Captain von Neidling was!

There was no choice. I took three quick steps and pressed my back to the wall beside the office door.

There was silence in the office. Then I heard a whisper. "Take your gun!" There was an ominous click like my .22 hunting rifle makes when I put a bullet into it.

My heart pounded as I watched the doorknob twist. The door opened suddenly but nothing happened. Slowly I saw the tip of a pistol emerge.

Can you imagine how scared I was? I barely managed to control myself. Then guess what happened? I pressed myself back more against the wall. For the first time, I felt something poking into my left shoulder.

It was the light switch!

I could see the whole gun now, but not the man. He was standing in the doorway. His other hand slowly appeared and began to move towards the light switch!

I squeezed sideways and hoped desperately that I wouldn't knock any more shovels over. The man's fingers fumbled for the switch. The tip of his finger brushed my shirt as he flicked it on.

Suddenly there was a noise on the far side of the room as another shovel fell over.

The whole room jumped as the gun went off. I was frozen in terror.

All the other men in the office shouted.

Then a cat jumped up onto the workbench and looked at the door. Laughter echoed out of the office.

"Did you shoot my cat?" demanded Captain von Neidling.

"No," said an embarrassed-sounding voice.

"So you missed?" said Captain von Neidling coldly. "That's even worse."

I was staring at the man's gun. A whiff of smoke was coming out of the barrel. The cat was sitting on the workbench. It was big and black, but I noticed its tail had a white tip. Its eyes looked enormous in the light. It looked at me for a second, then at the man with the gun. There was a funny look in its eyes as if it knew what it was doing.

The man slowly lowered his gun. "I hate cats," he said.

"And the cat knows it!" laughed one of the voices from the office.

The cat seemed to smile almost. He flicked his white-tipped tail playfully. Suddenly, my eyes widened. The tail was brushing against a nail in the wall. On it was a shiny new key!

Suddenly the man flicked out the light and the office door closed with a slam.

I was letting my eyes adjust to the darkness when I noticed a crack between two boards in the wall. I put my eye to the crack and realized I could see into the office.

I wanted desperately to run away, but I tried to control myself. "Just two more minutes," I said. I looked through the crack. Captain von Neidling's back was towards me. I was glad about that since it would have been too scary to look into the room otherwise. He was sitting at a table with a bunch of other men. Some I recognized from the Star Mine as friends of Black Moran.

Like Colonel Steele had taught me, I tried to remember as much as I could. I memorized the face of each man, how many moustaches there were, who wore hats and so on. There was a gun on the table plus Colonel Steele's bag, his razor and some socks. His books had been ripped page from page as if they were looking for something secret in the spine of the book.

There was a table close to the crack. I crouched down and looked through a knot hole in the wood to get a better look. It was covered with work papers from Star Mine. There was also some graph paper covered with scribbled numbers beside a book. I couldn't read the title but could see that it had a bunch of old sailing ships fighting with cannons on the front cover. Underneath was another book, but I could only read the start of the title *Alaskan Geology and the*—. The rest was blocked by the sailing ship book. I strained my eyes to read some of the scribbles but couldn't make anything out.

I realized I had better get going before the meeting ended. I let my eyes adjust to the darkness again. Then I stepped quietly across the floor. I rubbed the cat's neck for a second, then grabbed the key. Very, very carefully I clicked the lock open. Then I stepped out and relocked the door.

I was about to run off when I realized I had the key in my hand. If I took it with me, they would realize someone had been inside. I quickly slid the key back under the door on the side where it would have fallen if it had been knocked off the nail. Hopefully that wouldn't make anyone suspicious.

Then I took off down the alley, picked up Yves and we ran back to the hotel. As we ran up the stairs, we found Maman standing in the hallway tapping her watch.

Chapter 12

Telegram from London!

===

"Alaska War Jitters: Teddy Roosevelt Says He's Not Bluffing"

—Newspaper clipping from Mr. Taylor
July 21, 1903

The next day on the train back to Whitehorse, I sat beside Aurore and told her all about our adventure in the garage.

"Did the president really say he wasn't bluffing?" she asked.

"You bet," I replied.

"But Percy thinks he *is* bluffing!" We looked at each other for a minute. How could we get a message to Colonel Steele and Percy? And how could we make them believe it?

It was Aurore who had the idea. "Percy thinks Agent Y1 is an adult. Why don't we pretend to be Agent Y1 and send him a message!"

It was a bit chilly in the railcar, so we took a log out of the conductor's woodpile at the end of the car and put it into the woodstove. Then we clustered around to write our message.

"Who should we make it to?" I asked. "Percy?"

"You mean Piccadilly, his code name!" said Aurore.

"Right. And we should send it to Colonel Steele using his code name too!"

Aurore quickly wrote up our message. I knew I would have to do a lot of math to put it in code, so I told her to take out all the words we didn't really need. Then I encoded it just like Percy had taught us.

To Bull Moose and Piccadilly,
President Roosevelt came on secret fishing trip to Alaska last week. He got a forty-five pound King Salmon in ocean off Skagway, plus a two hundred pound halibut. Up Chilkoot Trail he shot small black bear and four grouse. Overheard him say privately he was not bluffing about attacking Canada with U.S. Army. Especially if Star Mine on border has a lot of gold! Many Senators in Washington own shares!! Oskar von Neidling and Thursten Vanderbilt III from rich family in New York also there. Thurston owns shares in Star Mine. Neidling and his gang stole Colonel Steele's briefcase.

With all due respect,
Agent Y1

PS No moose at this time of year. President says he might come back this Fall with his new gun and shoot one.

Actually, Aurore didn't write the entire message. I added the bits about the fish and moose hunting as I was encoding it.

"Kip, do we really have to put in the kind of fish he caught?" asked Aurore as she watched over my shoulder.

"Of course!" I exclaimed. "That's really important." Even smart girls like Aurore don't understand these things sometimes.

The first thing we did back in Whitehorse was go see Dad. He was feeling better and wanted to hear about President Roosevelt and Colonel Steele's briefcase.

When he got tired and went to sleep, I took the message to the Telegraph Office. I had a job there delivering messages and they were surprised that I wanted to send one! Especially one in code! It was expensive to send it to London. It cost me almost a whole week's wages! The operator told me it had to go 10,000 miles across Canada and on underwater wires under the Atlantic Ocean!

I sat by the window and watched him tap the message in Morse Code. Dot, dash, dot, dot and so on. If I had sent the message in the mail, it might have taken weeks to go by train to Skagway, ship to Vancouver, train again to Montreal and then finally ship to London. Instead, with a telegram, it might just take a few hours or even just a few minutes! It was funny to think that operators would be repeating my message in Telegraph Creek, Vancouver, Calgary, Winnipeg, Toronto, Montreal, Halifax and London and that sometime soon some boy in London would be running it to a fancy building where Percy would be getting his copy of Kim down from the shelf to decode it!

Life seemed to go back to normal. It was like the trip to Skagway never happened. School ended and all my friends went to do interesting things down the river or out in the bush. Two boys from school went mining in Dawson City with their fathers. Another went prospecting after his uncle heard Tagish Charlie found some gold near Kluane Lake.[1] My friend Jack was away working on the sternwheeler S.S. Canadian. I felt pretty sorry for myself. All I did was lug heavy suitcases to and from the hotel and run around town delivering telegrams.

If I had any spare time, Maman would make me chop wood and deliver it to Dad's customers. She said it was never too early to deliver wood for next winter and earn a little money while Dad was getting better. He told us he felt pretty good. His head looked a lot better, but he could still hardly walk because of his leg.

---

1.   Editor's Note: Tagish Charlie, along with Skookum Jim and George Carmack, sparked the Klondike Gold Rush by finding gold in 1896 on Rabbit Creek (later renamed Bonanza Creek). During the summer of Kip's story, Tagish Charlie did it again with a discovery on Fourth of July Creek. More than 2000 claims were staked, with Silver City mushrooming into existence on the shores of Kluane Lake.

I didn't tell anyone, but I was worried about him. Even moving around the house on his crutches seemed to tire him out. He looked pale and like he was about to faint. Despite that, he insisted on getting up. He even tried to go outside and chop some kindling for the fire, but Maman caught him and made him give me the axe and sit down.

He didn't say anything. He just looked sad.

Sometimes when I didn't have any bags to carry at the hotel, I would sit and think about that day at the Star Mine. Was it my fault? Did I bang a crate of explosives when I dropped the boxes? If I had helped unload the boat more instead of throwing rocks, maybe we would have been gone by the time the explosion happened. And why didn't I shout to Dad that Yves and I were safe. I'm sure he was running around looking for us when that rock hit him.

When I talked to Aurore about it, she didn't agree with me. "Don't be stupid, Kip! You got Yves to a safe place in the boat. If you'd gone out to look for Dad you just would have been hurt or killed too!" But I still thought about it a lot.

In the evenings, after dinner, Maman would make us play a game called Encyclopaedia. Each person had to pick a letter, then find the right Encyclopaedia volume and look up something interesting. Maybe "giraffe" in the "G" volume or "dynamite" in "D." Then you would tell the family about your word and they could ask you questions.

One time I picked the word "prison" and described it as a place where you had to chop wood, carry suitcases and read encyclopaedias. Maman didn't like that very much. But I could tell Dad thought it was pretty funny.

Sometimes after the dishes were done, we would gather around the dinner table and spread out one of the London newspapers that Aurore got from Mr. Taylor. They were always a few weeks old by the time they got to the Yukon, but Maman would make us translate some of the stories into French for her.

At first you think newspapers are boring, especially if you live in the Yukon. Everything is so far away! Who cares if France wants to capture Morocco but the Emperor of Germany has sent his navy to interfere?[2]

But then I read a story about a speech President Roosevelt made about Panama. It must have been just after he got back from Alaska. The United States wanted to build a canal across Panama so ships could go from the Atlantic Ocean to the Pacific Ocean without having to go all the way around South America. But Panama was actually part of a country called Colombia and the Colombians were stopping the canal. The newspaper was talking about President Roosevelt sending the U.S. Navy to take over Panama and build the canal.[3]

It made you think about our border dispute with Alaska and what President Roosevelt told me about "walking softly and carrying a big stick!" It was worrying. Maybe a war really was going to happen!

We would also cut out any stories about the Alaska boundary dispute. The Canadians, British and Americans all sent papers with their side of the story to the Tribunal of judges who were going to make the final decision and end the argument about where the border was. The British and Canadians were upset because the Americans had named people who weren't really judges and had already made up their minds in favour of the United States.[4]

---

2.   Editor's Note: Kip is referring to the early stages of the Morocco Crisis, which pitted France against Germany. Although both sides pulled back from war, the Morocco Crisis began a series of events that would eventually lead to World War One.

3.   Editor's Note: In July 1903, tensions grew in the Colombian province of Panama as the Colombian and American governments were unable to agree on building the canal. A few months later, President Roosevelt and the United States assisted a local junta in a revolution that made Panama independent and allowed the canal to proceed. The junta's ambassador Philippe Bunau-Varilla lived in the Waldorf-Astoria Hotel in New York, where he wrote the new country's declaration of independence and constitution, and designed the flag.

One evening, when we complained that nothing interesting ever happened, Maman announced that she would invite our teacher Mr. Galpin over for dinner the following night. She said that Dad liked his stories. I was horrified!

But once he got there it was kind of fun. He told us about his trip to Vancouver and all the plays he saw. He even asked me if I wanted to help make the swords for the school Theatre Club's next play, *The Merchant of Venice*.

But the best part was during dessert. Mr. Galpin was asking Maman in French (he's our French teacher too) if I was keeping up with my reading over the summer. I could tell he was expecting to find out that I hadn't even opened a book. But suddenly Yves interrupted with one of those sudden ideas he gets. "Do you think there will be a war with the Americans about the border, Mr. Galpin?" he asked.

Mr. Galpin was surprised. "The Vancouver newspaper doesn't think so," he said and patted Yves on the head.

"But that's probably what they said before the Spanish and American war five years ago," I replied. "You know, the one where President Roosevelt and the Rough Riders captured San Juan Hill."

"And if that caused a war, then I think either Panama or the Alaska boundary could cause another one," added Aurore.

"The London Times said exactly the same thing," I pointed out.

Mr. Galpin's mouth hung open for a minute with his fork in the air beside it. "Looks like you kids already have an 'A' in history for next year!" he said finally. When he repeated it in French, Maman and Dad smiled proudly. Dad was never taught how to write and he's always pleased when we do well in school. Then he elbowed me

---

4.   Editor's Note: When the British, Canadians and Americans agreed to set up the Alaska Boundary Tribunal, they agreed to appoint "impartial jurists of repute." Instead, President Roosevelt appointed two U.S. Senators and his Secretary of War to represent the United States. Tensions rose significantly as a result.

softly in the ribs. "If you can hold your temper in school this year," he whispered with a smile, sort of joking and sort of not.

Then Mr. Galpin gave us a copy of the Saturday Evening Post from June 20. "Look at this story!" shouted Aurore. "It's by Jack London ... remember the story teller we met in Skagway?" The story was called *Call of the Wild* and was about a Southern dog who has lots of adventures during the Gold Rush.

Above: Mr. Galpin and the Whitehorse school theatre club in costume for The Merchant of Venice, as mentioned by Kip. Bill Taylor is seated on Mr. Galpin's right. (Photo courtesy of the Bill & Aline Taylor collection)

"Look at the picture!" cried Yves. "It looks just like D'Artagnan!"[5]

5.　Editor's Note: Kip is referring to the scenes in *Aurore of the Yukon* when Aurore and Yves meet Jack London in Skagway and tell him the story about their dog D'Artagnan, who bears remarkable similarities to Buck in *Call of the Wild*. Previously, literary historians had believed London had used a dog in Dawson City as the model for the dog Buck. The *Saturday Evening Post* serialized *Call of the Wild* over several issues in the summer of 1903.

We read the story eagerly, but the magazine had only printed Part 1! We would have to wait a few weeks for Mr. Galpin to give us the next part.

There was lots of other stuff that was interesting in the papers that summer. They had a bicycle race in France called the Tour de France. It was 1500 miles long! France and the Yukon are about the same size, but we don't have a single paved road!

There was also a story about a man called Mr. Wright in Kitty Hawk, North Carolina who was planning to build a machine that could fly. Imagine if you could fly to Dawson City in a few minutes instead of taking five days on the sternwheeler. Now that would be amazing! "It'll never work," said Mr. Galpin, but I hoped it would.

The summer went along like that for quite awhile. Sometimes I would see Jack when the S.S. Canadian came back to Whitehorse. He looked sharp in his uniform and had lots of stories from Dawson City. It seemed pretty exciting, especially compared to carrying luggage and reading the newspapers at night.

Fortunately, my Dad was getting a bit better every day. I would take him some fresh pie or something, and then he would let me eat it as we played chess.

He was beginning to walk again. I knew that he and Maman argued about it after we went to bed. She kept telling him to rest since the doctor didn't think his leg was healed, but he kept saying he had to get back to work.

One day in July, I was sitting in the Telegraph Office. It was a slow day. I had my mini chess board and the London Times from Mr. Taylor. I was reading about the famous chess match at the Monte Carlo tournament in France between the grand masters Tarrasch and Maroczy. The newspaper listed the moves one-by-one so you could recreate the game. I sat there for a long time scratching my head, trying to figure out why they made this move or that one.[6]

The operator was staring dully out the window with his earphones on. Suddenly, he sat upright. "Wow!" he exclaimed. "Priority message! Clear the lines!" This meant a super important government message was coming. He started writing it down. I found the spare earphones and plugged them in. It was slow enough for me to follow so I scribbled down the message too as the dots and dashes came in.

I looked down at my paper as I was scribbling. "237237 XDFF DKD OSK DDNEJAK FIADR DR A DD."

"I'm getting the Morse Code all mixed up! It doesn't make any sense," I exclaimed.

"Quiet!" hissed the operator. "It's all in code!" He recopied the message onto one of the official forms, folded it in half, addressed the envelope, licked it and handed it to me. "Deliver it right away, Kip. It's urgent!"

I looked at the envelope. It had my name on it. "Deliver it to who? You're supposed to write the receiver's name on it, not the delivery boy's!" I said with a laugh.

The operator snatched it back from me. He looked puzzled. He looked at the envelope, then at his note pad. I looked over his shoulder: "To Kip Dutoit Urgent."

"It is for you!"

"Yahoo!" I said. "I hope I give myself a big tip!" I could hear the operator still shouting questions as I ran out the door.

---

6.   Editor's Note. The 1903 Monte Carlo international chess tournament was noted for its drama, especially when Russian master Mikhail Chigorin accused Prince Dadian of Mingrelia of cheating.

Chapter 13

Sternwheeler Surprise

"Alaska Boundary Dispute Heats Up: U.S. and Canadian Delegations Leave for London"

—Newspaper clipping from Mr. Taylor
August 16, 1903

Papillon was reading *Kim* to Yves when I got home. They were at the part where Kim goes on his first secret mission for Mahbub Ali. They clustered around as I took *Kim* and used it to decode the message from Percy.

MESSAGE NUMBER 1
TO AGENT Y1 URGENT
WE CANNOT BELIEVE NEIDLING WOULD STEAL SAM STEELE'S BRIEF-CASE. DO YOU HAVE PROOF? SUGGEST YOU RECRUIT MORE AGENTS. DON'T UNDERSTAND YOUR CODE NAMES KING SALMON AND HALIBUT. PLEASE CLARIFY. REPORT SOONEST.
PICCADILLY
END

Piccadilly was Percy's code name. Aurore looked at me and raised her eyebrows. "I told you not to put in all that stuff about all the fish that President Roosevelt caught. Now Percy thinks 'King Salmon' is someone's code name!"

"And he doesn't believe us about Captain von Neidling either," I said.

Yves ignored us both and grabbed the message. "Spiffo!" he shouted. "Percy wants more agents. Can I be one too?" I looked at Yves and Papillon and then back at the message. This was beginning to go too far! Percy didn't know that "Agent Y1" was just us kids and now he wanted Y1 to find more agents to spy on Mr. Neidling.

What were we going to do now?

Suddenly the gate banged in the yard. Dad was walking very slowly up the path. Maman was holding his arm. He looked like he was really in pain. He'd been walking for a few weeks, but he'd never looked this bad.

It turned out Maman had made Dad go back and see Dr. Nicholson again because his leg was still hurting so much. Maman looked very upset. "Votre père a besoin d'une opération. C'est beaucoup trop cher. Nous n'avons pas assez d'argent!" she sobbed.

It turned out Dad had been working too much. He had strained his leg and his leg bones had healed wrong. He needed a special operation and the Whitehorse Hospital couldn't do it. He would have to go to Vancouver, but almost all of our family's money was gone.

There was lots of bad news in Whitehorse that night. There had been a fire at Jack's house. The kitchen and roof were burnt completely away. Jack wouldn't be able to go on the S.S. Canadian's next voyage.

There was one good part to the story, though. Jack and the steward from the ship came to my house and asked if I could be ship's boy on the next trip to Dawson City! I could tell that Maman was not really happy with this, but I translated for Jack and the steward as they explained the job. The captain even stopped by and told Maman that he would take good care of me.

So I borrowed my father's leather bag and put my things in it. I took my chess set and a notebook to write a journal in. I had to leave *Kim* with Aurore in case more messages arrived, but I snuck the letter 'G' from our encyclopaedia set, as well as the latest section of *Call of the Wild*. I figured Jack London would like the idea of me reading it as we floated down the Yukon River.

Maman made me take warm clothes and my rain jacket even though Jack had told us that the ship's boy gets just one drawer for his things.

Jack's uniform was a bit too big for me, but I put it on anyway and ran down to the ship. It was kind of scary to walk up the gang plank onto the ship all by myself.

I almost forgot my Dad's operation—almost—during all the excitement. Soon the paddlewheel started turning and the crew untied the ropes holding the ship to the dock. There was cheering from the passengers on the deck and everyone on shore waved. I could see Maman waving a handkerchief. She was crying. I think Aurore, Papillon and Yves were crying too. I waved back and tried not to cry.

Then the ship's bow, which is what they call the front, turned into the river. Suddenly the whole ship felt alive. The Yukon River is so powerful you could feel it grab the ship and turn it around. The deck pulsed with each turn of the paddlewheel. I caught a smell of the wood smoke from the smokestack—thick and black—and felt the spray from the paddlewheel. Then one last cheer as we headed downstream and my family got smaller and smaller on the dock.

I think I would have stood there a long time, when suddenly I heard a shout from the steward. "Kip! Cup of tea to the captain! Be smart about it!"

That was his way of saying "Fast!" so I ran to the kitchen as quickly as I could.

The ship's boy had all kinds of jobs. I had to get up early and help the cook make breakfast. I had to take many, many cups of tea up to the Captain in the wheelhouse! Have you ever carried hot tea up a ladder? It's not easy! The first time I spilled so much that there was only one mouthful left in the Captain's cup by the time I got there!

Above: Kip was ship's boy on the S.S. Canadian, seen here nearest to the camera drawn up on shore for the winter in Whitehorse. (Photo courtesy of MacBride Museum 1989-3-066)

The Captain was usually very good to me. The only thing that got him angry was spilled tea. After a few trips, I got better getting up the ladder. Then I had an idea. I put a bit of cold water in the tea to cool it. At the bottom of the ladder I would take a huge sip and hold it in my mouth. Then, I would run up the ladder. At the top, I'd spit the tea back into the cup.

It was genius. The captain said I was the best ship's boy he'd ever had!

I decided not to tell him about my secret though.

After taking morning tea to the captain, I had to help in the restaurant serving breakfast to everyone. Then it was cleaning up the passengers cabins and making the beds. In the afternoons I had to change out of my fancy uniform into work clothes and help in the engine room. It was unbelievably hot and noisy. There was one guy called a fireman whose only job was to put a four-foot-long log into the boiler every minute or two. The ship used up a huge amount of wood, sometimes two cords of wood per hour! A cord is a stack of wood four feet high, eight feet long and four feet wide. It was amazing to watch a pile almost as tall as me, as wide as my arms and as long as my bed disappear into the furnace every 30 minutes!

We always seemed to be stopping to load more wood.

I had to help the engineer too. He was always fixing something. I had to get tools, hold things while he hammered them with a huge hammer, or clean up grease. I also had to run to the Pitman arms. These were the giant beams that made the paddle wheel turn. I had to pump fresh grease onto them several times every day to make sure they didn't seize up.

I liked the noise and activity, but it was scary too. With so much steam and so many big moving parts, it would be easy to get hurt if you didn't watch out.

In the evenings, I had to help the cook again. Every night there would be a huge pile of potatoes waiting to be peeled. It took forever, although one night I got off easy. A passenger on holiday from Seattle had been asking me about Yukon cooking all day. Especially the moose roast we were cooking that night. When I ran into him on my way to the kitchen, I asked him if he wanted to help cook the moose. He did, of course, and he was so happy talking to the cook that he didn't notice that he peeled most of the potatoes! "This is the life!" he would exclaim, each time I opened a new bag of potatoes for us to peel.[1]

Then I would serve dinner to the passengers in the fancy dining room. Then I helped with the dishes. After that I would try to read, but I was usually too exhausted and just fell asleep! I slept so hard that I never heard the crew changing shifts in the middle of the night!

---

1.   Editor's Note: Kip wasn't the only ship's boy to think of this trick. Yukon pioneer Laurent Cyr used to tell a very similar story about his days as a young boy on the S.S. Klondike. As the Klondike was a much bigger ship, he would have had even more potatoes to peel than Kip.

My first trip to Dawson City went so fast it seemed like a blur. It only took about a day and a half because you have the river current pushing the ship along. But I hardly remembered the trip back to Whitehorse either. It takes four or five days, but I seemed to either be working or sleeping the whole time!

Kip and Louis throwing rocks on the sternwheeler

Louis

Kip

CANADIAN

aurore
1903

Above: A drawing by Aurore of Kip and Louie throwing rocks on the sternwheeler S.S. Canadian.

But I had the hang of it by my second trip. That time, there was another boy on the boat too. It was Louie from Teslin, the boy who had brought us grayling in Whitehorse after Dad got hurt. He was travelling with his father down the river. While they were on the boat, his dad was helping move the firewood from the back of the ship to the fireman. His father also took turns as the fireman.

Louie would help his old man move the logs. It always looked kind of funny since Louie was about my size and could carry just one four foot log, but his dad used a giant trolley that could move twenty of them!

The first morning Louie and I were too busy to talk to each other. I could tell he was a fun fellow though, because when adults weren't looking he would pick a very light log and pretend to stagger like it weighed 1000 pounds! He was very funny.

At lunchtime, I took my food up to the bow. Going downstream on that part of the river they don't have to use the winches or poles, so it was practically the only quiet part of the ship.

Louie was already there. He had a rock in his hand. I could see him looking at a log floating in the river. He pulled his arm back and then threw. He was a good shot! The rock bounced right off the middle of the log! "Bullseye!" he shouted.

"Good shot!" I said. "Too bad there aren't many rocks on this ship!"

I sat down beside him. He told me that his dad was going to work on the ship for a trip and then they were going to get off at Fort Selkirk and rejoin their family. Fort Selkirk is about halfway between Dawson City and Whitehorse.

We sat on the side of the ship and chatted. I'll never forget my feet dangling over the side of the ship as the water rushed by. Every once in a while the bow would hit a wave and some spray would land on your face. The air was cool and crisp and the trees on the shore went by like magic. Sometimes, we'd see some ducks or maybe a moose munching weeds in the shallow water near the shore.

"Better eat your lunch, Kip! Engine room duty in twenty minutes!" shouted the steward. That woke me up! I was starving. I opened my handkerchief. The cook had made me a canned ham sandwich. It looked great. I could see Louie looking at it too. I didn't see what he was eating for lunch, so I offered him half my sandwich.

We ate fast. I don't think boys generally talk when they eat.

But when we were done, and Louie and I had finished my apple, he said, "I wouldn't be so sure there aren't any more rocks on this ship!" He smiled and opened the bag he had been holding. It was full of rocks! They were perfect for throwing. "I filled it up in White- horse before we got on the ship," he said.

He gave me three. "See that stump on the shore?" I said. "Five points to the guy that can hit it first!" My rocks were pretty close. But one of Louie's hit it right on top and bounced into the forest.

Suddenly the ship's whistle blew. We looked up at the wheel- house. The Captain had been watching our contest and had blown the whistle. He gave us a thumbs up sign. "Good shot! Next time get us a duck for dinner!" He shouted with a smile.

Sometimes I got a break in the late afternoon, too. After I had fin- ished in the engine room, they gave me time to clean up and have a snack before going to help the cook. Louie and I would go to the bow and throw rocks at logs or other targets. I really wanted to throw a piece of firewood in the river to shoot at, but the fireman told us he'd put us in the boiler instead if we did that.

When we stopped to get more wood, I always had a million jobs to do but Louie would dash onshore and find more rocks.

We were on the way back on my second trip when we stopped at Fort Selkirk. My job was to carry the passengers' bags off the ship if they were staying in Fort Selkirk, or to carry the new passengers' bags onto the ship.

"Get them on board, then look at the tags and put them in the right cabin," said the steward. I ran down the gangplank as he shouted after me. "And make sure you stack them neatly!" I carried two fancy suitcases on board and looked at the tag: "Kapitän von Neidling."

I almost dropped it into the river in surprise. It turned out that Captain von Neidling and his son Rudi were joining us. They had one of the First Class cabins.

We were soon chugging along again. Going upstream was much slower. The engines were really working and made the deck vibrate constantly. The fireman also had to work extra hard loading wood into the boiler and the stacks of firewood seemed to disappear off the decks in no time.

I was standing on the bow beside Louie when I saw Captain von Neidling. He was up in the wheelhouse talking to the Captain. Another of Louie's throws had hit the target. He reached down to the bag of rocks on the deck and took another. Suddenly Rudi appeared beside us.

Rudi slapped me on the shoulder in a friendly way.

"You don't have to play with that Indian any more," he said. "Come up to my cabin and I'll show you my dad's new gun. It's the new Colt pistol. It holds two more bullets than a six-shooter!"[2]

I really wanted to see a gun like that. He seemed to naturally expect that I would listen to him and leave Louie. I looked at Louie. He was looking down at the rock in his hands and fiddling with it. It slipped through his fingers and bounced into the river. He looked sad.

"I think I'll stay here." I said. "With my friend Louie." I slapped Louie on the shoulder like Rudi had done to me a minute before.

Rudi's eyes narrowed. With a quick kick, he knocked Louie's bag of rocks over the side. "Hey!" I shouted.

But Louie grabbed my sleeve. "He's a passenger. You'll get in trouble."

Rudi smirked. "You'll be sorry, Indian-lover," he said. Then he walked away. He said the words "Indian-lover" like it was a really bad thing.

I looked up at the wheelhouse. Captain von Neidling had been watching the whole time, but his face was expressionless. I looked into his eyes for a moment and wondered what he was thinking.

---

2.   Editor's Note: Presumably the Colt M1900, precursor to the famous U.S. Army Colt .45.

That evening in the First Class dining room I had to serve the von Neidlings. Rudi seemed to enjoy making me run back and forth to his table. "My milk doesn't taste right. Get me another," he said. He bathed every bite in ketchup so he could send me back for another little dish of it. He dropped his fork three times. "Dad, does that boy look funny to you? I think his uniform is the wrong size," he said loudly as they were eating dessert.

He was really making me mad. I was thinking about "accidentally" spilling something on him. I think the steward noticed. He pulled me aside and whispered in my ear. "Kip, don't do it. He's not worth it. Just grin and bear it!"

It was pretty good advice. I took it. Each time I was sent for more ketchup, I just tried to smile more. It really seemed to make Rudi mad.

I was relieved that they were almost done their meal. I went to another table and collected all the dirty plates and put them on a big platter to carry to the kitchen. It was a big load. I was passing the von Neidling's table when, suddenly, my foot caught on something. I teetered, then fell down! As I went, I saw Rudi pull his leg back under his chair.

I fell right in the middle of the corridor. Plates smashed everywhere. Worst of all, a half full soup bowl landed right in a woman's lap! "My dress," she cried.

I jumped up. Rudi was sitting very properly in his chair. As for me, I had spaghetti on my jacket and stew on my hands. Everyone was staring at me. "He walks funny too, Dad!" said Rudi with a smirk.

I haven't been that mad very many times. I wanted to beat Rudi von Neidling to a pulp!

I moved to jump on him. I don't think Rudi was expecting me to fight back because he suddenly looked alarmed. But when I tried to move forward, I found I couldn't! The steward had quietly but firmly put his hand on my collar.

Suddenly Rudi was brave again. "Better pick up your mess!"

I looked up into the steward's eyes. His look said, "Are you going to clean up this mess or do I have to drag you out of here by the ear like a five-year-old?"

"Sir, let me get the mop," I said. I apologized to the woman while the steward promised to get the dress cleaned.

I was still on my knees cleaning the floor when the von Neidlings left. "Can't expect much more from local boys, I suppose," said Captain von Neidling.

Chapter 14

Triple Urgent for Kip Dutoit!

"Alaska Rumor: President's Friend Tells British He's Not Bluffing!"

—Newspaper clipping from Mr. Taylor
August 16, 1903

It turned out to be a good thing that the steward had stopped me from tackling Rudi von Neidling in the First Class dining room on the S.S. Canadian.

If he hadn't there's no way I would have found myself in the von Neidling cabin the next day. The steward sent me there to tidy the room and fix the beds. You could tell he wasn't sure he could trust me alone in the von Neidling's cabin. I knew it because the first thing he said to me was, "I know I can trust you, Kip."

He made me look him in the eye and shake his hand and promise not to do anything to Rudi. "Remember! No dead muskrat tails in that boy's bed!" he said as I left the room with the broom and duster.

The von Neidling's cabin was last in the row. I finished making the bed in the special way the steward had shown me. He said that the covers were supposed to be tucked in so tight that a nickel would bounce if you dropped one on them. I've never understood the point of bed making since you just mess it up again at bedtime. But it seems to be an important part of ship life.

Rudi had left his stuff laying all over the room, so I had to put his shoes in neat pairs by the door and pick up the clothes he left on the floor.

Then I started dusting. The cabin had a little writing desk in it so you could write postcards to your friends. Captain von Neidling had some books out on the desk. I was dusting them when I suddenly recognized the sailing ships fighting on the cover. It was the same book he had out on the desk in his secret office in the garage in Skagway!

It was called *The Naval War of 1812* and was actually written by President Roosevelt! I remembered Colonel Steele telling us that President Roosevelt had written a lot of books before he became president.

This was getting interesting. I quickly closed the door to the cabin. I stood with my duster in the air so that I would look like I was dusting if anyone came in unexpectedly.

There was another book underneath. I could only read part of its title: *Alaskan Geology and the–*. I reached down to move the top book and see the rest of the title when my hand froze.

I remembered back to that scary night in the garage in Skagway. That time, the sailing ship book had been in exactly the same place on top of *Alaskan Geology*.

I remembered how Colonel Steele always left his things in a special pattern so he could tell if anyone had been spying on him. Was Captain von Neidling doing the same? Why?

I carefully memorized where everything was on the desk, especially how *The Naval War of 1812* exactly covered up the last words in the title of the book underneath. Then I slowly opened the book. A single spruce needle slid off the word *War* in the title onto the desk. "Was that a coincidence?" I wondered.

The book looked like Captain von Neidling had read it often. The pages were well worn and had quite a few dirty finger marks. But the most interesting thing was the inside cover, which had words in a foreign language.

I picked up the pencil, remembering that it had been on the corner of the desk pointed exactly at the lamp, and wrote the inscription on a scrap of newspaper I had in my pocket (the hockey scores section, actually, which I had sneaked out of the First Class lounge).

Here is what it said:

> *An meinen kühnen Kapitän, der, treu und furchtlos, den Rühm der deutschen Kriegsmarine durch die ganze Welt verbreitet hat.*
> *Wilhelm*

What did it mean? And who was Wilhelm and why didn't he have a last name?

I carefully lifted up the book to see if any papers would fall out. None did, but I noticed small pencil marks on some of the pages. Other than that, the book looked normal. I could see the last two words of the title of the book underneath, which was called *Alaskan Geology and the Border Mountains*. There didn't seem to be anything special about it.

I stuffed the paper into my pocket, put the pencil back (pointing right at the lamp, of course), put the books back in the right place and carefully put the spruce needle back on the word *War* on the cover.

I was about to leave when a sudden thought came to me. If I was supposed to dust the room, wouldn't I knock the spruce needle off the book? If it was still there, would Captain von Neidling wonder why I hadn't dusted it off? I decided to leave the spruce needle there. It was better that he think that I was a lazy duster than that he get the idea that I might have been snooping in his books.

If, of course, he really was the kind of guy who put spruce needles on books to see if anyone was snooping. It could just be a coincidence.

As soon as we had unloaded in Whitehorse, and I had got blisters on my hands from dragging the von Neidling's unbelievably heavy suitcases to the hotel, I ran home to find Aurore, Papillon and Yves.

Believe it or not, they were all sitting around the kitchen table doing math homework.

"Did I come back to the right house?" I asked in amazement. They looked up in annoyance at me. What was going on? Who could be so upset that their math homework was getting disturbed?

Then I noticed the book *Kim* in front of Papillon. She was copying a sentence onto graph paper.

"Two telegrams from Percy in one day!" exclaimed Yves.

"He sent them on Tuesday and Saturday last week but they got held up at Vancouver and delivered here both on the same day," said Aurore. I pitched in and started reading the letters to Papillon and Yves. Aurore did the math. She suddenly seemed to be better at math than she usually claimed. As she wrote out the two messages, I could see they were in that strange telegram style with words missing to save money.

> MESSAGE NUMBER 2
> TO AGENT Y1 VERY URGENT
> STILL NO NEWS FROM YOU. WHO STOLE SAM STEELES BRIEFCASE?
> LIKELY NOT NEIDLING. IS KING SALMON A LOCAL CHIEF? COULD
> HE HAVE STOLEN BRIEFCASE?
> PICCADILLY
>
> MESSAGE NUMBER 3
> TO AGENT Y1 VERY URGENT
> CONFIRM RECEIPT OF THIS MESSAGE. YOUR SILENCE WORRYING. IS
> KING SALMON HOSTILE? WHY WOULD HE STEAL BRIEFCASE?
> PICCADILLY

"We decoded his last message but I guess we never sent him anything back," I said.

"I had chores to do," said Yves. "It's your fault."

GOVERNMENT TELEGRAPH SERVICE,

Form No. 2 x
35,000-19-6-1902.

DEPARTMENT OF PUBLIC WORKS,

DOMINION OF CANADA.

The following message was received by the Government for transmission, subject to the terms and conditions printed,
which terms and conditions have been agreed to by the sender.

12. W. FE. H.   17 Paid

London 8 Sept. 1903.

Kip Dutoit,
          White Horse, Y.T.

011.011. KWHZAEZ DJRPOZ CC.
          MESSAGE NUMBER 3
FH DKIXK S.AA. KORR SDNVBD. SHCMDI LDZZIPD AH
TO AGENT Y I. VERY URGENT. CONFIRM RECEIPT OF
LDHX MASQSDG. ROED PZOCXDZ JZHHXYUF. JZ PURD WWQSID
THIS MESSAGE. YOUR SILENCE WORRYING. IS KING SALMON
ODBCHUR? ITT OWPLD HW DDTUR HGUOADPOE?
HOSTILE? WHY WOULD HE STEAL BRIEFCASE?
          YFFHSEUTYC
               PICCADILLY

Above: A unique 1903 telegram found with Kip's scrapbook. It appears to
be the actual sheet he used while decoding one of Percy Brown's
messages. Fortunately for historians, he ignored Percy's instructions to
burn all copies. Keen readers will note how Percy encrypted the numbers,
which Kip forgets to explain when he describes book codes in the story.

"What chores?" I said. "I'm the one that cuts all the wood around here." Yves always acts like he does all the work, but of course he's the littlest and can't even lift the big wood splitting axe!

"Stop bickering, boys!" said Aurore.

"Percy sounds worried," said Papillon. "We should send him a message."

"And we better tell him that King Salmon is really just a kind of fish," added Aurore pointedly. "Somehow Percy has got it into his head that someone code named King Salmon stole the briefcase instead of Captain von Neidling."

Suddenly there was a bang as someone knocked our front gate open. It was the Telegraph Office's other delivery boy. He bounded up the front stairs and pounded on the door. He was puffing furiously and had a letter in his right hand.

Between breaths he told us the story. "Letter ... puff ... for Kip ... puff ... Triple Urgent ... puff puff ... never had one of those before ... puff ..."

I snatched it from his hand and left him still puffing on the doorstep. I did the math furiously as Aurore read the letters to me.

I could hear the boy calling to us from the porch once he got his breath back. "Hey Kip? Who would send you a telegram anyway? And in code?" I crossed out a math error. He was distracting me. "Did you send it to yourself to look like a big shot? I bet you did! Ha! Ha! Kip Dutoit getting big shot coded messages like Captain von Neidling!" He laughed uproariously again like this was the funniest thing he'd ever heard.

I couldn't do the code math with him shouting at me like that.

"Hey Papillon," I said in annoyance, "go kick him in the shins and tell him to get lost."

We paused for a second. I had my pencil poised in the air. Aurore had her finger under the next letter in *Kim*. Yves ran over to the window to watch.

We heard Papillon open the front door.

"Hi Papillon," said the delivery boy.

"Don't make fun of my big brother!" she said. There was the unmistakable sound of a girl's shoe connecting with a shin bone.

"Ouch! What was that for?" Then another kick. "Ouch! Ouch! All right! All right!" Then footsteps, the front gate slamming shut, and the sound of D'Artagnan's barking as the delivery boy ran out of sight.

I started doing the math again and read the message.

TO AGENT Y1 TRIPLE URGENT
WORRIED YOU ARE VICTIM OF ENEMY ACTION. IF I DON'T HEAR FROM YOU IN NEXT TWENTY FOUR HOURS WILL ARRIVE WITH REIN-

FORCEMENTS SOONEST. PLEASE SET UP EMERGENCY MEETING WITH
KING SALMON WHEN I ARRIVE.
PICCADILLY

"Oh no!" exclaimed Aurore. "Percy's going to come to the Yukon
if we don't send him a message!"

"He'll find out there's no Y1 for sure! And he'll want to meet someone named King Salmon."

"All right. I'll write him a message," I said.

"About what?" asked Aurore.

I told them what I had learned on the ship.

"Write a telegram to Percy saying that Captain von Neidling has
a book with a German inscription we don't understand? That's not
very big news," pointed out Papillon. She was right. We had to find
out something more.

Yves still was standing by the window. He looked thoughtful. "The
delivery boy said Captain von Neidling is getting coded messages
like us," he said. He turned to us. "Is he a spy too?"

Suddenly, I knew. "How could I be so thick!" I exclaimed. "The
book with the inscription ... it's for a book code! That's why Captain
von Neidling always has it with him."

"I know what we have to do," said Aurore. "First, translate that
inscription. Second, get hold of Captain von Neidling's next secret
message and decode it!"

We all agreed. "And we'd better get cracking. Maman won't be
shopping at Taylor & Drury's forever," pointed out Yves.

Chapter 15

Who is Kaiser Wilhelm?

"Alaska Border: U.S. and Canada Putting Together Final Arguments"

—Newspaper clipping from Mr. Taylor
August 24, 1903

"I know how to figure out that inscription!" I said. "There's a German-English dictionary at school. I'll go ask Mr. Galpin."

I grabbed the scrap of paper with the inscription on it. I hopped our fence into the alley. The usual kids were playing there and called to me to join them. "Later!" I shouted and ran past them towards Mr. Galpin's house. I jumped up his steps in one bound and rang the door bell.

He opened the door, looked at me, and glanced over my shoulder down the street. "Hello Kip," he said guardedly. That's a word Aurore just taught me. It means he wasn't happy to see me but he wasn't angry either. He just couldn't figure out if I was there to deliver something, ask for something or to play a trick on him.

I told him I needed the key to the school because I wanted to learn some German words. His eyes narrowed and he looked at me suspiciously. "Sorry, Kip." He said. "Better wait till school starts." I could tell he was thinking about the time I got mad at Rudi and knocked the bookshelf over.

"Please?" I begged. Mr. Galpin put on his teacher's face. I knew the answer would be no.

I also knew that if Aurore or one of the other "good" kids in school had asked, the answer would have been yes.

I was very frustrated. I trudged home, kicking rocks along the way. A squirrel ran up a tree by Mr. Taylor's house. It scolded me from a branch just out of reach. Even the squirrels were mad at me. I snatched a rock angrily and threw it as hard as I could at the squirrel.

It chirped in fright and leaped for cover. The rock just missed it.

Unfortunately, the rock kept going right past the squirrel and over Mr. Taylor's fence. I heard the sound of smashing glass and a shout: "The tomatoes!"

Above: Behind the family home on Steele Street in Whitehorse. Kip describes running down this alley on his way to Mr. Galpin's house. (Photo courtesy of the Bill & Aline Taylor collection)

"Dang!" I cursed. "Stupid rock!" Mr. Taylor was famous for his greenhouse. He worked at it all the time and could even grow tomatoes, which are about as rare as camels in the Yukon. I've only ever had canned ones, but I guess fresh ones must be delicious considering how much time Mr. Taylor put into them. He even planted them in the spring in his living room and moved them outside when it got warm enough.

Anyway, I just had time to dive behind an enormous rhubarb plant when the gate flew open. It was a good thing that rhubarb grew so well in the Yukon. I crawled under the leaves and hoped Mr. Taylor wouldn't look too hard.

As I lay there, I asked myself a bunch of angry questions. Why did that squirrel have to pick that branch to stand on? Why did Mr. Taylor have to build his greenhouse right there? Why did the rock have to be such a stupid shape? If it had been rounder my throw would have been better. And why did rhubarb have to be so wet?

Then I calmed down a bit and remembered what Colonel Steele once told me. "Don't blame the dogs for being slow if you overloaded the sled." It was his way of saying there was no use in blaming other people when you made a bad choice.

Then I got mad at myself for getting mad. I could hear Mr. Taylor go back into his yard and close the fence.

This was really getting stupid, I decided. I realized I was mad at myself for getting mad at myself for getting mad at the squirrel, the rock and Mr. Taylor's greenhouse.

I stood up, walked to the gate, and knocked. "Mr. Taylor, I threw that rock." He twirled around and stared at me and the rhubarb like we had just magically appeared. His mouth dropped open slightly. He didn't say a thing. "I didn't mean to hit your greenhouse, sir, but I'll replace the glass with my own money."

It felt good somehow, even though I knew there would be consequences.

Mr. Taylor didn't seem to know what to say. "Thank you, Kip," he said finally. "Looks like the tomatoes are fine." It was almost like he was treating me like an adult. I think if he had caught me hiding under the rhubarb he would have had a mighty temper.

By the time I got home Papillon had come up with a better idea to get the German words translated. "Why don't we ask Mr. Lieb-herr?" said Papillon. "Remember how he said he owed us after we found his dog last summer?"

I remembered that. When Papillon heard that the Liebherr's dog was missing, she had made a bunch of "Lost Dog" posters. She dragged us all out to look for it. At the time, I wanted to play with Jack and I don't think I was very nice to Papillon for coming up with the idea.

But we found the dog and Mr. Liebherr was very happy.

And when we arrived at his shack it was tied up outside. It jumped up on Papillon and licked her face as soon as it saw her.

The Liebherrs' cabin used to be a wall tent, but Mr. Liebherr had gradually covered it with bits of wood. When he got married and Mrs. Liebherr had a baby, he added a room on the back made mostly of packing crates. The walls were covered with words such as "Fragile," "This end up," or "Farmer Johnson's Canned Milk." If you didn't look carefully, you might think it was just a pile of junk. But then you'd see the little windows and chimney. Mr. Liebherr was just flat-tening a tin can to nail over a hole in the roof when we got there.

"Wow!" he exclaimed when he saw us. "All four of you. This must be serious business!"

We went inside and I showed him the scrap of paper. You could tell he was happy to be asked about his native language.

"It's very fancy German," he said. "It says: '"To my bold captain, who, loyal and fearless, has spread the glory of the Germany Navy throughout the world.' It's signed by Wilhelm." He pronounced it "Vill-helm."

"And who is Wilhelm?" asked Papillon.

Mr. Liebherr laughed. "Who is Wilhelm! Why he's the Kaiser of course!" I wondered what a Kaiser was, but I didn't want to ask since Mr. Liebherr seemed to think everyone should know.

But Papillon asked. "Mr. Liebherr, what's a Kaiser?"

Mr. Liebherr laughed again. "That's right, Papillon. If you don't know, ask! No such thing as a dumb question." He took a sip of tea. "Kaiser Wilhelm would be very upset to find out that you don't know who he is. He thinks he is the most famous ruler in the world. Kaiser is German for Emperor. This is signed by Kaiser Wilhelm, or Emperor Wilhelm of Germany!"

Papillon winked at me. I knew what she meant. If I was as nice to Mr. Galpin as she was to Mr. Liebherr, my life might be a bit easier.

Anyway, we all patted the dog, said something nice about Mr. Liebherr's new roof patch, and then ran back to Main Street as fast as we could.

We ran right into Louie at 3rd and Main Street. He had three grayling for Maman.

"Captain von Neidling really is a German Navy captain!" I exclaimed.

"And a friend of Kaiser Wilhelm!" said Papillon.

"And a German spy!" said Yves.

"Holy Smokes!" said Louie in amazement. He stared at me as I told him the whole story. Then he thought about it for a minute. I could tell he was thinking about what a beast Rudi had been to him on the boat. Finally, he said, "Well, I guess we better figure out a plan."

Louie was right. One of the passengers on the sternwheeler had given me a dime as a tip, so we went to the Taylor and Drury store and got a big bag of hard candy to suck on as we thought up our plan. Maman said we couldn't afford "luxuries" and hadn't bought us candy in weeks.

There was a newspaper on the counter in the store. I could see the headline: "International Tribunal's Decision on Alaska Border Expected Soon."

I grabbed the candy and we headed for the bank of the Yukon River to figure out what to do. "Whatever Captain von Neidling is going to do, it'll be soon," I said as I gave everyone a red gobstopper.

The planning was hard. We had to figure out the answer to a very tough problem. We needed to get information to send to Percy, including proof that Captain von Neidling was a German spy.

We could try to listen to one of his meetings, but it might be in German. And I had learned the hard way in Skagway how hard it was to get near one of his meetings with guys like Black Moran walking in and out.

Or we could try to decode the coded messages we knew he was getting, but we would have to get both the messages and his special code book. That didn't sound too easy.

Or we could try to get one of his gang to tell us Captain von Neidling's secrets. But did any of his gang even know all the secrets? And how could we get one of them to talk to us?

And if we didn't figure something out, Percy would come back to the Yukon. Not only would he find out Agent Y1 didn't exist, but I knew adults well enough to know that Percy might come up with any number of crazy and dangerous schemes of his own.

"We could ask Maman to take us on a long fishing trip until everything's over," suggested Yves.

Everyone laughed. "You saw the newspaper," I reminded them. "We have to do it now."

Finally, we came up with a plan. My part was first. And it was the easy part. I gulped.

Chapter 16

The Plan

<hr style="border-top: 3px double;" />

"You look guilty boy. Got anything to confess?"

—*Black Moran, in my journal*
August 24, 1903

I walked up to the Telegraph Office. I needed to get into the files where they kept copies of old messages. They always kept them for a few months in case the delivery boy took it to the wrong place. I pushed open the door.

The operator said hello. He looked bored. I knew I couldn't just ask to go through the files. Everyone's messages were supposed to be private. That means that the people at the Telegraph Office aren't supposed to read them for fun and find out everything about you.

I knew that's what the operator did sometimes anyway, even though he wasn't supposed to. But he wouldn't let me do it.

I could offer to do the filing of today's messages, but since I didn't get paid for that it would make the operator suspicious.

So I decided to take advantage of my reputation as a boy who is often in trouble.

I looked sheepishly down at the floor. "I delivered a message to the wrong house. The other operator told me I had to come in and do your filing."

We both looked at the pile of messages that needed filing. The operator had nothing to do all day except send a few messages and do the filing. But he never seemed to get around to it.

The operator was delighted to give me his pile of filing. Whenever a message came in, they gave it its own number and entered the recipient and time of day in the log book. Then they typed the message on special double paper. It has two very thin sheets, with a black sheet of carbon paper in between so that you just have to type the message once and a copy appears automatically on the bottom sheet.

Then the delivery boy took the top copy to the customer. The words appeared on the bottom paper too. These went into a big pile. Every day the operator was supposed to put them in a folder for that week. Each folder had a special, bendy brass pin stuck to the back. You stabbed each message onto the pin. That way, they were all in order. At the end of the week, you bent over the top to hold all the messages in. Then you started a new folder for the new week.

I actually kind of liked the filing. The thin paper made a neat crinkly noise, and the smell of the carbon paper and files always reminded me of the interesting messages I had seen. You weren't supposed to read them of course, but you did. You found out who was expecting a baby, whose uncle had died and left them money, and who was leaving the Yukon for the winter. Some of the business telegrams had the words shown normally, but all the numbers replaced by letters. The operator said that Taylor & Drury used the word "Cumberland." It had ten letters and none repeated, so "C" was 1, "U" was 2 and so on. The bank used the word Manuscript, apparently.

I don't think Mr. Taylor or the bank manager would have been happy to hear that the operator knew what codes they were using!

And every once in a while you would see a telegram that was 100% garbled letters or all in code.

That's what I was looking for: coded messages that the operators couldn't read.

I started by filing. I moved slowly and watched the operator. I was waiting for him to have a nap or to start reading a book. Anything so that he wasn't paying attention to me.

After a few minutes, it happened. He asked me to mind the office for a few minutes so he could get a coffee. I knew he was really heading to the White Horse Hotel for a cribbage game with his friends, but that was fine with me.

I figured I had at least twenty minutes. I pulled open the drawer of old messages and pulled out the folder for last week. I quickly flipped through them. I was looking for any messages to Captain von Neidling or the Star Mine.

I quickly found copies of our coded messages from Percy. I ripped them out and stuffed them in my pocket.[1] I saw that Mr. Galpin's sister in Vancouver had just had twins. I reminded myself to focus on the job and not get distracted.

I found one to the Star Mine. It was message #87. But it was from a mining equipment company in Seattle. It wasn't in code and was complaining that a bill hadn't been paid. I flipped to the next message. I found a few more from a bank in Vancouver and an explosives company in Seattle. "No warranty or liability for past-date product," it said, whatever that meant.

---

1.   Editor's Note: This may explain why none of Percy's secret messages to Agent Y1 can be found in the Yukon Archives in Whitehorse, a fact that has puzzled historians and researchers from the Department of Foreign Affairs. According to Norman Penlington in *The Alaska Boundary Dispute*, Kip was not the only one trying to steal telegrams around this time. U.S. agents in Washington were also intercepting the British ambassador's telegrams. They could not decode the messages, so they instructed the telegraph company to scramble the coded letters so that the ambassador would be unable to read them. This forced the ambassador to rely on the diplomatic courier, who was slower than a telegram, or to use the regular mail which could be intercepted.

I flipped through some more messages. Then I noticed something. I had message #123 to Taylor and Drury, and then the next message was #125 to the Bank of Commerce. Where was #124?

I flipped open the log book and found it. "#124. Arrived 2:14PM. To Oskar von Neidling, Star Mine. From BA Import Export, Washington, DC.

But there was no copy of the message in the folder.

I soon found four other missing messages. My heart raced. Captain von Neidling must be up to something if someone is stealing his messages. Or, I realized, if he is making sure no one else could read them!

Then I went to the Diary file. This had copies of all outgoing messages that people had sent from Whitehorse to other cities. Whenever the operator was done sending a message, he would poke it onto a big brass spike sticking up out of his desk. The nail held the whole pile there until someone (usually me!) filed them at the end of the day.

I found the Star Mine messages to Seattle and Vancouver, each with a little hole in the middle from the brass spike. I noticed that Captain von Neidling hadn't responded to the ones about unpaid bills. But just like the incoming messages, the copies for the messages to Washington, DC were missing.

I was searching the last file when the door banged open. I almost leaped out of my pants. I had completely forgotten that someone might walk in.

It was Black Moran. He stood perfectly still in the doorway. Most people would have walked up to the counter and said hello. Instead, he just stood there and watched me. His eyes were as black as his beard.

"You look guilty, boy," he said slowly. "Got anything to confess?" I saw his right hand fidgeting by his belt as if it was looking for something. I remembered he didn't wear his six-shooter in Canada since the time Colonel Steele arrested him for it and made him chop a cord of wood at the police detachment.

"I confess you scared me," I said. I thought it was a pretty good come back. Anyway, he stared at me for another minute.

"Where's the operator?"

"Getting a coffee. He'll be back in 20 minutes."

Black Moran grunted. He pulled a crumpled piece of paper marked *White Horse Hotel* out of his coat pocket and got ready to copy his message onto one of the Telegraph Office forms. Whenever you sent a message, you had to write it down with the address on a telegraph form for the operator to read as he did the Morse Code.

He stepped over to the counter. "Hey, boy!" he said loudly. He tapped his finger on the counter.

"Yes, sir," I replied.

"You thick or something? You expect me to write a message with no paper in the pad?" He spoke to me like I was an idiot. "Get me a new one," he snarled.

I jumped to grab a fresh pad of telegraph forms. He began scribbling his message. I stayed at the counter. Without looking too suspicious, I tried to read his message upside down.

The address was to Berlin-Amerika Import Export Company. I watched eagerly as Black Moran scribbled the address in thick, bold letters. The first letter was "W" followed by "A" and "S." I watched the rest one by one. It was for Washington, D.C.! This was exactly the kind of message I was looking for. Pretending to tidy up the counter, I inched closer.

Black Moran wrote each letter carefully, checking back with his scrap of paper. The first letter was D, then B, then L and then U. It was a coded message!

Black Moran suddenly glanced up and caught me staring at the letters! He hissed viciously. There was a savage gleam in his eye. "Curiousity killed the cat. Genesis 2:6."

I remembered he liked quoting from the Bible, although I didn't remember the Bible saying anything about curious cats.[2] But I moved quickly away anyway. I picked up a broom and pretended to sweep the floor, starting with the part as far from Black Moran as possible. He continued scribbling onto the pad.

The operator came back with a smile on his face. I guessed he had won a few dollars playing cards with his friends at the hotel. Black Moran gave him the form and the operator tapped the message in Morse Code. It was too fast for me to understand, and there was no way to remember the random letters anyway.

Fortunately, I knew the operator would put the form into the file as soon as he was done. Then I just needed to grab it when the operator wasn't looking.

The operator finished the Morse Code, grabbed Black Moran's form and spiked it onto the pile with the rest of the day's messages. Black Moran opened the door to leave, but suddenly stopped halfway through. He turned suddenly and looked at me. Hard. "Hey, ain't you the boy Sam Steele took to Skagway?" There was a snarl in his voice.

Suddenly, as quick as a marten, he darted behind the desk and snatched his message from the operator's spike. "Share not your secrets with the unrighteous. Romans 2:14."

Black Moran stuffed the paper in his pocket and stomped out the door.

The operator looked at me as he turned to his typewriter. "He's got cabin fever," he said, twirling his finger beside his head. Cabin fever is when you spend the whole winter in your cabin in the bush and go a bit—or a lot—strange.

"Yeah, cabin fever ... without the cabin," I replied. Then I noticed something. The sun was getting low in the sky and slanting in through the Telegraph Office windows. It fell right across the desk. I blinked. I

---

2.   Editor's Note: It doesn't. Black Moran seems to have occasionally invented his own Bible quotes.

could see little shadows on the next sheet of the pad of telegraph forms. They showed where Black Moran had pressed his pencil when he was writing on the top sheet a few minutes before!

I grabbed the telegrams out of the "To Be Delivered" box, ripped the top telegraph form off the pad, and dashed out the door.

"Those are important! Be careful!" shouted the operator as the door slammed.

"You're more right than you think!" I panted to myself as I ran up Main Street to find Aurore and the gang.

Chapter 17

Happy Birthday Princess Viktoria Luise!

===

"Alaska Boundary Dispute Heats Up: Tribunal Meets Face to Face in London"

—Newspaper clipping from Mr. Taylor
September 3, 1903

I gave Yves my telegrams to deliver. As I dashed home, I could hear the little wheels on his wagon rattling as he ran down the boardwalk to the first address.

Holding a sharp pencil sideways, I shaded the telegraph form. Sure enough, Black Moran's thick, bold letters began to show up.

"DBLU ..." It was definitely in code.

"Time for our plan!" said Papillon. "We're ready!"

We looked up to see Louie pelting across the street with Yves close behind. "The Neidlings just arrived for dinner!" panted Louie.

Papillon and Aurore loaded their things into Yves's wagon. One was a small spruce tree that Papillon had cut down with Dad's axe a few minutes before.

"Are you sure you can keep the Neidlings busy for long enough?" I asked. I have to admit I was nervous.

"Yes!" said Papillon. "We have prepared a long program ... a very, very long program!"

"But how can you be sure he'll sit through it?"

"Kip, just leave it to your sisters!"

We arrived at the White Horse Hotel and took up our positions. The girls and Yves went into the hotel and started talking to the front desk clerk. Yves poked his head out the door and gave us the thumbs up sign. That meant the Neidlings were in the restaurant.

Louie and I dashed around back of the hotel to where Captain von Neidling's room was. It was on the upper floor. Louie stood on a log and I stood on Louie's shoulders. I pulled out my father's fishing knife and slid the long, thin blade under the window to find the latch. Slowly I began to work the latch.

I could see the latch wiggle as the knife touched it, but then Louie's log wobbled. I teetered and looked down. I could see all the junk in the hotel's backyard. An old wood stove. Old chimney pipes. A chair. All kinds of painful looking things.

"Hurry up!" hissed Louie. He was a strong guy, but I guess I was heavy. I slipped the edge of the knife under the window sash and tried again to jiggle the lock. I could see it move, but I couldn't quite get it to click open.

Louie slipped and the knife almost slipped out of my hand. "Faster!" he gasped. It was getting darker.

"Calm down! Try again," I whispered to myself. "It's moving … almost got it … one more try …" The lock popped open. I quickly pushed up the sash.

Suddenly, I heard a window open underneath me. Louie froze. So did I. Then I heard a voice. It was one of the cooks from the hotel. It meant trouble.

"Hey! No Indians allowed!" the cook shouted. "Get outta here, boy!" he shouted again at Louie. I guessed—or hoped—he couldn't see me on top of Louie's shoulders.

Louie didn't move. He was giving me time to climb into the window. I saw the cook's arm come out of the window and reach for Louie. "Don't make me come out there, boy!" shouted the cook. Louie still didn't move.

I gripped the window sill, put my foot on the top of Louie's head, and catapulted myself into Captain von Neidling's room. I looked back out the window just in time to see Louie sprinting up the alley with the cook chasing him with a broom.

There was no way the chubby cook would ever catch Louie, so I turned around and scanned the room. All the clothes were carefully hung in the closet. Captain von Neidling's sword was there too. The beds were made. There was a table with business papers, a type-writer and rock samples. There was also a small box that looked like it had just been opened. Inside there was a bottle of chloroform, just like I'd seen at Dr. Nicholson's. Interesting, but I didn't have time to waste so I kept looking around.

Then I found what I was looking for. On the desk, as I'd hoped, was Captain von Neidling's book *The Naval War of 1812*. I was about to grab it, but I stopped myself in time. There was a spruce needle sitting on the word "War."

This was just like when I had seen the books in the von Neidling cabin on the sternwheeler. Also like before, *The Naval War of 1812* was sitting on top of Captain von Neidling's other favourite book, *Alaskan Geology and the Border Mountains.* The top book exactly covered up the words "Border Mountains" on the cover of the book underneath. A pencil sat on top pointing right at the lamp. I smiled. Captain von Neidling was definitely a spy!

I set the pencil and spruce needle aside, pulled the telegraph form from Black Moran out of my pocket and opened the book. All I had to do was decode the message now!

I just hoped I had enough time. Papillon and Aurore were sup-posed to keep the von Neidlings in the dining room. Their plan was to wait until the von Neidlings were almost finished dinner, then to rush in and sing songs for them. Sort of like how we went caroling around town at Christmastime. But I wasn't so sure it would work this time. After all, Captain von Neidling didn't seem like the kind of guy who liked children's singing.

Suddenly, I heard Papillon's voice.

"Ladies and Gentlemen, tonight we are pleased to present a medley of German songs in honour of Princess Viktoria Luise, daughter of Kaiser Wilhelm of Germany. Today is her 11th birthday!"[1]

"Yes!" I exclaimed. Papillon was a genius. That was why she was looking up the German Royal Family in our encyclopaedia. There was no way the von Neidlings would walk out in the middle of songs in honour of a German princess!

I heard laughter and men's voices. "Sit down, Neidling!" said one. "I'll tell Kaiser Wilhelm if you leave now!" called another loudly.

I heard my sisters begin to sing Silent Night. In German! I couldn't believe it. They told me later that it was originally written in German and that their piano books had the original words.

Anyway, I quickly turned to the book. Like Percy had explained to us earlier, a book code like ours or Captain von Neidling's is very easy once you know which page and sentence to start with.

I felt myself go red in the face and there was a twisting feeling in my stomach. We hadn't thought of that when we were making our plan. I had no idea what page to use! The clock ticked loudly on the wall above the desk.

What would I do? I read the coded message looking for a number. But there was just letters! "Don't panic," I told myself. "Just figure it out!"

I heard the girls start a version of "O Christmas Tree." Even I knew this had a German version called "O Tannenbaum." They were singing it about as slow as you could. I took a deep breath and turned back to the book.

I read the message again, looking for anything strange. I noticed that the first word was DBLU and that the last word was DBLU. I remembered something the telegraph operator once told me.

---

1.   Editor's Note: Assuming Papillon had the dates correct, this would place these events on Sunday, September 13th, 1903. Princess Viktoria Luise was the youngest of the German emperor's seven children.

Since telegrams get repeated by each station as they go along, it's easy for spelling errors to get made. That's why if you really want to make sure a word gets through, you repeat it twice.

I stared at the letters. DBLU. DBLU. DBLU.

Were they numbers somehow? D could be 4 and B could be 2. But L was the 12th letter and U was the 21st. Was it code for the number 421221? But what did that mean?

Then it hit me. The letters were all in the word "Cumberland!" I remembered what the telegraph operator had told me about the code Taylor and Drury used. "Cumberland" had ten letters and none of them were the same. Perfect for a number code. I realized Captain von Neidling was using the same code as Taylor and Drury!

In "Cumberland," D was the 10th letter, B was 2nd, L was 7th and D was the 4th.

0274!

I looked on page 2 for line 74 but there weren't that many lines on the page.

Then I checked page 27 and looked at line 4. The book was written by President Roosevelt and I could almost hear his voice as I read the words. "To the north we are still hemmed in by the Canadian possessions of Great Britain."[2]

The next word of the telegram was ZPFV. I wrote this on my paper and then underneath I wrote the first four letters of the sentence from the book: "To the north" so the first four letters were TOTH. My pencil flew as I did the math. The letter "Z' was 26, minus 20 for "T."

---

2.   Editor's Note: This can be confirmed as a true quote from Theodore Roosevelt's book. Captain von Neidling appears not to have chosen the code-sentence at random. The full sentence reads as follows: "To the north we are still hemmed in by the Canadian possessions of Great Britain; but since 1812 our strength has increased so prodigiously, both absolutely and relatively, while England's military power has remained almost stationary, that we need now be under no apprehensions from her land-forces; for, even if checked in the beginning, we could not help conquering (Canada) in the end by sheer weight of numbers, if by nothing else."

That equaled six. The first letter was "F!" I did the whole word. It was "FALL."

I had cracked the code! I scribbled down the rest of the words I needed from page 27 and began doing the math. Add, subtract, carry, scribble. The words were German and some didn't make sense. But enough did that I knew I had the code working right.

I was halfway done when O Tannenbaum ended. I heard more shouts. "Come on, Neidling. Don't be a sourpuss!" Another man called out, "What would the Princess say?"

Then Papillon's voice. I think she knew she could keep him there for just one more song. And it had to be a good one. "Now we will sing Happy Birthday to Princess Viktoria Luise. Everybody please stand and join in."

I began to sweat. Happy Birthday wasn't a very long song.

"Slowly, with royal dignity!" shouted Aurore. "Thanks sis," I said to myself as I scribbled away.

I was almost done when the last verse died out. Papillon cried out, "Captain von Neidling, make a toast to Princess Viktoria Luise." There were shouts of approval from the other diners in the restaurant. I could hear Captain von Neidling clear his throat. I scribbled even faster.

I dashed down the last letter. I looked quickly at the decoded message.

FALL AEOL WIE VEREINBART BIS ZUM 27 SEPT BEREIT. GELD FUER GOLDKAUF ERHALTEN. WERDE FRUEH MITTEILEN, DAMIT ALLES IN WASHINGTONER ABENDPRESSE ERSCHEINT. BRAUCHE NOCH HUNDERT DOLLAR UM ZU VERSICHERN, DASS ES GANZ OBEN IN DER SKAGWAYER ZEITUNG ERSCHEINT. BOREAS.

What did it mean, I wondered. And who was Boreas? Then I heard glasses tinkle and chairs scrape as everyone stood up. Then heavy footsteps in the hallway.

I was too slow! I jammed the papers in my pocket and closed the book. I quickly began rearranging things. *The Naval War of 1812* on top, just covering the words *Border Mountains*. Pencil on top, pointed at the lamp. I picked up the spruce needle when I heard a key in the lock.

Panic! What would I do now?

Then I heard Yves's voice. "Captain von Neidling! I love you!"

I heard sounds of scuffling in the hallway.

Then Rudi's voice. "Hey kid, let go of my Dad's leg! He doesn't want a hug from you!"

There was more scuffling. "Huggy huggy!" shouted Yves.

I put the needle back on top of the book and bounded for the window. I slid my legs through, found a toehold underneath and reached up to pull the window shut. Just as it shut, I felt my toes slip. I fell backwards.

"The junk!" was all I could think as I hurtled down into the White Horse Hotel's backyard. I landed with an enormous crash on a pile of old chimney pipes. They clanged like a brass band. I quick rolled under an old canoe just as I heard the window open. My head banged into a pile of burlap sacks marked "Star Mine." "What are these filled with? Rocks?" I muttered to myself as I squirmed out of sight.

"Who's out there?" shouted Captain von Neidling.

I looked out from under my canoe to see Louie hiding under the back stairs beside the hotel's cat. He winked at me, then picked up the cat and threw it out onto the chimney bits I had just landed on. The cat landed with a clatter and scrambled onto an old wood stove.

I heard Rudi's voice. "Don't worry, Dad. It's just a cat."

Chapter 18

The North Wind Starts to Blow

"Alaska Tension Grows: London Tribunal to Vote on Border Soon"

—Newspaper clipping from Mr. Taylor
September 14, 1903

Ever had to sit politely, eat little cakes and talk about the weather just to be polite?

It's bad enough when your mother makes you do it at Christmas time when Father John visits in the middle of a street hockey game. But it's pure agony when there's a real spy on the loose!

We were at Mr. Liebherr's house to ask him to translate Captain von Neidling's telegram. But he was so happy to see us that he invited us in for tea. Aurore had already kicked me under the table twice when I tried to blurt out what we wanted.

When he stood up to get the tea water off the stove, she turned to me and whispered, "Kip, we can't just barge in here demanding things. Be nice!" Mr. Liebherr returned with the teapot.

I opened my mouth to speak, but before any words could come out I felt Aurore's boot connect (again) with my shin.

"Something wrong, Kip?" asked Mr. Liebherr.

"Err ... oh, just about to say thank you for the tea," I replied. I hadn't been hurt falling out of Captain von Neidling's window. But I was sure that I now had a nasty bruise on my shin.

Aurore smiled sweetly as Mr. Liebherr poured her cup and gave her another German cake. She picked up her tea cup with her little finger in the air, just like Queen Alexandra of England. "And how are your dogs? Ready for the winter?" she asked Mr. Liebherr politely.

I couldn't take it any more.

"Mr. Liebherr!" I gasped. The words shot out of my mouth like a mouthful of tea that's too hot. "We really need your help! Can you translate this for us?" I slammed the telegram on the table.

Aurore smiled. "You know boys, Mr. Liebherr. Out of control!" She sounded just like Maman.

Mr. Liebherr smiled, found his reading glasses and began to read. "Operation Aeolus ready here for Sept 28 as requested. Money for gold purchase received. Will send news early to make evening newspapers in Washington. Need 100 dollars to pay Skagway news-paper for front page coverage. Boreas."

Mr. Liebherr looked quizzically at us over the top of his reading glasses.

"Is 'Aeolus' a German word?" asked Aurore. I could tell she was trying to be as innocent as possible.

"No," said Mr. Liebherr. "I don't suppose too many Yukon trappers know this, but then again not too many Yukon trappers went to the Berlin Academy. Aeolus was the Greek god of the winds. You know the story of the Trojan War? Well, when Odysseus was on his way home from the war Aeolus gave him a magical bag that had all the winds in it. Odysseus was supposed to let out a bit of the West Wind—slowly—to help blow his ship home. But the men on the ship opened the bag when they weren't supposed to. They were too hasty." He looked at me and smiled like a grandfather. "Too out of control."

"And what happened?"

"All the winds got out! There was a huge storm! Bigger than any human had seen before! Odysseus was blown off course and didn't get home for ten years!"

"And who was Boreas?" asked Aurore.

"One of the winds. The North Wind, in fact." He looked at us again. "A rather strange fellow to be sending a telegram, don't you think?"

We all looked at each other in silence.

"Is this a real telegram?" he asked.

"Err … just a school project," I said. "Thanks for the cakes. Very, err, German."

"Danke schön," said Aurore. Of course she knew how to say thank you in German.

We put on our boots and shook hands. He looked at me with his eyebrows raised and a faint smile. As we walked across his yard he called out, "And be careful, children. In Greek times, Boreas was a dangerous enemy."

We walked home. We were both deep in thought. "Do you think Captain von Neidling is 'Boreas?'"

"He must be. Who else would sign a telegram like that? Black Moran can barely read! And he would call himself Ishmael or Joshua or something biblical."

"What does Boreas have planned for September 28th? And why does he need to pay the newspapers?"

"Whatever it is, it can't be good! We'd better send another message to Percy."

That night we re-encoded the telegram with *our* code and sent it to Percy. The next day after school another Triple Urgent message arrived for us.

We had hoped that responding to Percy's message would keep him happy in London. But instead, it had panicked him into coming anyway.

I bounded back downstairs after decoding the message. "Percy and Colonel Steele are coming!" I rushed into the kitchen full of excitement.

All the other kids were sitting around the table. But no one looked at me. They were all staring intently at their after school snacks.

I saw why. Maman had that look in her eye. " Kip, pourquoi es-tu le seul garçon au Yukon qui reçoit des télégrammes 'Triples Urgents' de Londres? Est-ce que le roi d'Angleterre est un ami spécial?"

"Non, Maman," I said. When she asks questions like whether you're getting telegrams because the King of England is a special friend, you know you're in trouble.

"Donne-moi le télégramme, s'il te plaît." I gave her the telegram. Aurore, who was behind Maman's back, mouthed the words, "You blew it, big mouth!"

Maman read the telegram. "We arrive September 27. Piccadilly." She seemed puzzled. Disappointed even. "Le colonel Steele arrive le 27 septembre? Avec Piccadilly, ce monsieur anglais ridicule?"

As soon as we were done our snack and were back upstairs, Aurore kicked me in the shin again. "You idiot! I'm glad Percy didn't put anything incriminating in that telegram! Fortunately Maman thinks Percy is an idiot."

"She's right!"

"Well, you're lucky he didn't put anything in the telegram about burgling Captain von Neidling's hotel room or bribing newspapers in Alaska! We can't afford to be grounded on September 28th."

"Yeah!" said Papillon. She kicked me in the shin too.

I have to admit that I deserved it.

The next few days were the longest of my life. School seemed to drag on forever. I tried to get Mr. Galpin to teach us some German, but he just laughed and got out the Latin books. Every day after school, I would run down to the White Horse Hotel and the Telegraph Office. I carried suitcases from the boat to the hotel. From the train to the hotel. From the boat to the train. From the hotel to the train and the boat.

I delivered boring telegrams about babies, bank loans and birthday greetings.

Nothing seemed to happen. Rudi was the usual kind of nuisance at school. Captain von Neidling, however, wasn't his usual energetic self. He just seemed to be enjoying himself around town. He had late breakfasts and long coffee breaks. It was like he was waiting for something.

In fact, he almost seemed bored.

That is, until someone got word from the Golden North in Skagway that they were putting on a big costume party on September 28th. This seemed to galvanize Captain von Neidling. His usual energy came back as he dashed all over town looking for a costume that would fit him.

We tried to keep track of him, but it was impossible. First we heard that he had been to the Clarke's for a pair of white pants. Then at the North West Mounted Police post looking for brass buttons. Then getting something from Whitehorse Laundry. I was picking up some sewing for Maman at Taylor and Drury's when I saw him come in. I quickly ducked behind the curtain into the back room where no one could see me.

Captain von Neidling piled a bag of clothes onto the counter. "Can you have these sewed in time for the Golden North party?" he asked.

The clerk looked through the bag. "You're going as a waiter?"

I expected Captain von Neidling to explode.

Instead, he smiled. "No, I'm going as an admiral. I'm planning on having the best day of my life, so I might as well dress up."

"Admiral who?" asked the clerk.

"Admiral Nelson, the British hero of course!" Captain von Neidling was almost cheery.

"Didn't Admiral Nelson get shot?" asked the clerk.

Not even that bothered Captain von Neidling. He just smiled and explained everything to the clerk. "And a second identical costume for my son Rudi," he concluded.

A few minutes later, Captain von Neidling was gone. "More sewing for your mum," said the clerk as he gave me Captain von Neidling's bag. "Don't mess it up or he'll kill me!" he shouted as I left.

As soon as I got home, I ripped open the package. Sure enough, there were two pairs of white pants, two blue jackets and two white shirts.

I asked Aurore about the party and the costume as Maman started sewing. "The party's on September 28th too, just like Operation Aeolus. It can't be a coincidence!"

"Maybe it can," she said. "If Captain von Neidling knew about it in advance, he wouldn't be running all over town looking for his costume!"

We also saw Black Moran when he was visiting from the Star Mine. He would sit in the hotel restaurant whispering to Captain von Neidling. Or they would go up to Captain von Neidling's room. Black Moran was on his best behaviour. He pretended not even to notice me. Once he was even happy enough to whistle a few tunes as he walked back to the train.

During this time, Captain von Neidling received two telegrams. Unfortunately, Black Moran snatched the papers and I couldn't figure out how to get a copy. Not that I wanted to sneak into Captain von Neidling's hotel room again, anyway!

He also sent a telegram. I got a copy of that, but it wasn't even encoded. It was to the Golden North Hotel in Skagway: "Reserve two rooms for night of party. Tell mayor not to dress as Admiral Nelson this year. Neidling."

When I got home, I asked Aurore if she thought it could be a code. "Maybe," she said. "Or maybe the whole thing is just a joke and there's nothing special about the 28th at all."

Meanwhile, we were receiving a shower of telegrams from Percy. It was all right if they came after school, because then I was supposed to deliver them to myself. But if they arrived during school hours, Maman got them.

She started opening them of course. But since they were in code she couldn't understand them. She even went down to the Telegraph Office to complain about the quality of their telegrams, but fortunately no one there speaks French so they couldn't figure out what she was talking about.

It was a good thing, actually. Even though they were grown-ups, they were kind of scared of Maman. Especially if she was wagging her finger in their faces and calling them "Monsieur." I knew how that felt. Anyway, after Maman's visit, they usually kept the telegrams until after school to give to me.

I just hoped they weren't giving a copy to Black Moran too!

The problem was that all of Percy's telegrams asked for more news. Who is Boreas? What is Operation Aeolus? Why is September 28th important? Can you recruit more agents? Is the Yukon cold in September? All kinds of questions.

We didn't have enough money to answer them all. And we didn't know the answers anyway! So I just sent one telegram back. "Don't know," it said. I gave up when Percy wrote back saying, "Don't know what?"

Finally September 27th came.

Maman smiled as we devoured our breakfasts and ran down to the station to meet Colonel Steele. "Il faut être poli à l'autre monsieur aussi," she reminded us, insisting that we be polite to Percy too.

As I arrived at the train station, I was surprised to find the manager of the White Horse Hotel looking for me. "C'mon Kip! We need your help. You wouldn't believe how much luggage the von Neidlings have this time!"

The White Horse Hotel's luggage room was full of suitcases and there was another pile of trunks near the front desk. They were covered with stickers from places with names like "Monte Carlo," "Biarritz" and "Deutsch-Südwestafrika."

The manager had a long list on his clipboard. He told me to take the trunks and suitcases across to the train. I looked at the huge pile. He laughed. "Yep. Looks like they're moving away."

"Today?" I asked. It was only September 27th and Captain von Neidling's telegram said Operation Aeolus, whatever that was, wouldn't happen until the 28th.

"No. The luggage goes today. They're not leaving until tomorrow … which reminds me … those bags of rock in the back are *not* supposed to go today." He made a note on his clipboard. "They're supposed to go on the same train as Captain von Neidling tomorrow morning."

We went upstairs to check if there were any more suitcases in the von Neidling's room. It was completely empty. They weren't leaving anything at the hotel like they usually did. Even Rudi's homework books were packed. The manager checked under the beds and in the closet.

"Good thing we looked in the closet. I almost forgot the sword!" he said. I grabbed it and took it downstairs. I remembered that Captain von Neidling always had his old sword from the German Navy hanging in his room. No one was sure if it was a real sword or just for special occasions. Rudi said that he had killed ten men in Africa with it. My friend Jack said that the only thing it had ever cut was a wedding cake.

Chapter 19

An Unexpected Train Ride

"U.S. Navy Ready for War with the British"

—*Newspaper clipping from Mr. Taylor*
September 14, 1903

Something was definitely going on. The von Neidlings had a huge pile of luggage. It looked as if they were leaving town and didn't plan to come back.

I ran back to the hotel to get the last few bags before Colonel Steele and Percy arrived. I was in the luggage closet when I saw Black Moran coming down the stairs.

He was dressed like Father John from our church! He had a black robe and white priest's collar.

Suddenly I heard Captain von Neidling's voice. "Moran! Excellent costume! You remind me of Cardinal Richelieu!"

"Who?" Black Moran didn't look too happy to be dressed up.

"You know! The French Cardinal who broke every rule in the book in the Three Musketeers!"

This didn't mean anything to Black Moran. "Well, it fits anyway. Should be a good party in Skagway tonight," he said unenthusiastically.

Through the crack in the closet door, I saw Captain von Neidling lean closer to Black Moran. "Especially for us, Moran! Nothing can stop Operation Aeolus now," he said softly.

Now I could see Captain von Neidling too. He was dressed like an admiral! He had a tight blue jacket, white pants and a fancy old-fashioned admiral's hat.

Rudi was right beside him and dressed exactly the same. The tailor from Taylor and Drury's was kneeling beside Rudi measuring his pants.

Captain von Neidling admired his costume in the lobby mirror. "I think I'll wear mine to breakfast." He grabbed Black Moran's arm and laughed. "Would you please join me, Father?"

I took the last few bags and crossed to the train. Then, with my hands sore from carrying luggage, I ran over to my sisters and brother to wait for Colonel Steele and Percy.

There were only a few other people on the platform, including one of Black Moran's henchmen. That's a great word Colonel Steele taught me that means "fellow bad guys." He was carrying a wooden case marked "Sekt." He put it down carefully beside the tracks and tapped the ticket agent on the shoulder. "Take personal care of that and make sure it gets to the Golden North for the party tonight. No 'breakage' if you know what I mean. It's von Neidling's favorite German champagne."

"Sure thing. Is Captain von Neidling celebrating something special tonight?" asked the ticket agent.

"You'll see," grunted the henchman.

Finally, the train came in. There were only two passengers on it. Not too many people plan to come *to* the Yukon just before winter I guess.

Colonel Steele stepped off the train first. "Well, if it ain't Sam Steele!" exclaimed the ticket agent. Black Moran's henchman almost jumped out of his boots. He stared at Colonel Steele in amazement.

Meanwhile, Percy stepped off at the other end of the carriage from Colonel Steele. Papillon pulled on my sleeve. "Look, Kip! He's pretending he doesn't know Colonel Steele!"

Sure enough, Percy was wearing a long trench coat and a funny hat. In fact, it was just like a drawing in that new book called *The Return of Sherlock Holmes* that I got for my birthday.

Percy walked over to the wall of the station. For some reason, he began to read the schedule that was posted on the outside of the station. Gradually, he moved towards us.

I tried to smile at Colonel Steele and act normally. But I couldn't help noticing Black Moran's henchman. His cold, blue eyes flitted back and forth between Percy and us.

Above: The railway station platform in Whitehorse where Kip saw Black Moran's henchmen slip onto Colonel Steele's train. Seen from the sternwheeler dock on the river. (Photo courtesy of MacBride Museum 1989-3-251)

Gradually Percy came closer. He leaned on the pillar just behind, but with his back to us.

"Don't turn around," he whispered. "This is Piccadilly. We need to speak to Y1 immediately. Has he found out anything about—" Percy looked over his shoulder. "About this fellow King Salmon?"

Colonel Steele pretended not to hear him. Instead he clapped me on the shoulder and shook my hand. As he did, he whispered, "I suppose everyone on the platform is staring at Percy and us right now."

"Yep," I said.

Colonel Steele sighed. Then he stood up straight, turned around and raised his hat to Black Moran's henchman. "Good morning," he said loudly.

The henchman eyed him suspiciously, but Colonel Steele ignored him and started walking towards the Arctic Restaurant. He grabbed Percy's sleeve and pulled him along. "Come on! Let's have a real Yukon breakfast. My treat. You too, kids!"

I looked back to see the case of champagne sitting alone on the platform and Black Moran's henchman running back towards the White Horse Hotel.

Percy complained for a few seconds that that Colonel Steele had ruined his disguise, but finally agreed to come along. "A cup of real coffee would be just the thing," he said in his fancy London accent. "I must say, chaps, the coffee on that train tasted like burnt tree bark."

Colonel Steele laughed. "That's because it really was burnt tree bark. Just the thing to perk up some coffee grounds you've used three or four times. Can't exactly go out to the corner store when you're trapped by a rockslide on the White Pass! Mind you, anything brown and hot with a bit of canned milk in it is good by me."[1]

Percy coughed and looked pale.

We were soon seated in the Arctic Restaurant, right beside the White Horse Hotel, with Colonel Steele devouring a huge plate of

---

1. Editor's Note: Early Yukoners had a wide range of coffee substitutes, including burnt chicory, Labrador tea and worse.

eggs, ham, bacon, sausage, hash browns, toast, not to mention a side dish of cold steak. Yves sat on his lap as he told us yarns from his mission in South Africa that made us howl with laughter, stopping only long enough to pop little pieces of ham into Yves's mouth.

It was like old times.

All the same, the Arctic Restaurant had big windows and I noticed that he had chosen a chair that had a perfect view of the train across the street. I followed Colonel Steele's eyes as he watched the train, the luggage and the people walking down the street.

I told Colonel Steele about what had happened. Unfortunately there wasn't too much to tell lately, since we hadn't decoded any more telegrams. Colonel Steele was interested in the luggage and how Captain von Neidling was leaving the next day.

The door banged open. It was three of Black Moran's friends. They sat in the corner and ordered breakfast. They didn't look at us, so I kept telling my story to Colonel Steele.

As usual, Percy wasn't paying attention to me. "I must say," he exclaimed, looking at his plate, "I'm not sure which is bacon and which is egg."

"Your stomach'll figure it out," snapped Colonel Steele, suddenly interested by something out the window. He turned to me. "Kip, what's in those burlap sacks?"

"Rocks," I said. After all, I thought, I had banged my head on them under that canoe.

"Yes, but what kind of rocks? Any tenderfoot yahoo can see they're rocks! But what kind of rocks? What did your powers of observation tell you?"

This was the old Observation Game we used to play with Colonel Steele. But it wasn't a game today. I cleared my throat nervously. "Well, it wasn't sand. I can lift a sandbag. I could barely move these and they're not all that big. And it wasn't gravel either. There were some big pointy rocks inside the bags. And there wasn't any of that grey dust on the sacks like when a silver shipment comes through."

"Hmm ..." mused the Colonel. "Good observation, Kip."

Then I remembered what the hotel manager had said. "But the manager told me the sacks of rocks weren't supposed to go until tomorrow!"

Out the window, I suddenly saw Captain von Neidling, Rudi and Black Moran carrying more burlap sacks across to the train. Captain von Neidling was waving his fancy admiral's hat as if to hurry them along.

If Colonel Steele was surprised to see Captain von Neidling dressed like an admiral, he didn't show it. You have to do better than that to surprise Colonel Steele.

Rudi and a few henchmen went onto the train, then Captain von Neidling. Black Moran was last. He hung out the door, looked suspiciously up and down the platform, then disappeared into the passenger car.

"They must have seen you arrive," I whispered to Colonel Steele. "They're leaving a day early!"

Colonel Steele looked at Percy, who continued to pick nervously at his breakfast. "Eat up, Percy. Train leaves in 3 minutes."

Percy's jaw dropped. "By Jove! You don't mean to suggest that we go back aboard? The cars are nothing more than rattling coffins with wood stoves!"

"I certainly do! Now drink the rest of your tree bark and let's go. Who knows what wily old Neidling might be up to in Bennett or Skagway. So let's tag along. You know, just an innocent trip to Skagway ... and a chance to keep an eye on the Captain. Who knows what we might find out!"

Percy stuttered. "B-b-but what about Agent Y1? Hadn't we better talk to him first?"

"Blast Agent Y1!" said Colonel Steele. "I bet Kip here knows just as much as Y1." I carried their two suitcases back across the street for them. As we walked, Colonel Steele put his hand on my shoulder. "You did a good job, Kip. Someday, you'll be able to come along on a trip like this."

Percy and Colonel Steele climbed onto the train. The conductor was already blowing his whistle. Aurore, Papillon and Yves stood on the bench on the platform and waved. I took the luggage to the luggage car. The conductor was out of sight, so I hefted the suitcases in through the open door. Just then I noticed Black Moran stick his head out of the front passenger carriage. As the train started to move, he looked up the street.

To my amazement, two of his friends from the Arctic Restaurant dashed silently but quickly across the platform and hopped onto the train. A third one raced afterwards, stumbling as he tried to tighten his belt.

"He's got a pistol!" gasped Papillon. She was right. He was strapping on his gun belt as he ran.

The train was still going slowly. The man jumped aboard.

"That was the door Colonel Steele used! They'll sneak up on him!" exclaimed Yves.

He was right. I had to warn the Colonel. The train was just starting to roll. There was no choice. I ran after the baggage car, reached through the open door and pulled myself aboard.

I was just looking for a place to hide when I saw Papillon's arms reach through the door. She swung herself into the car with Aurore right after her. "Hey!" I said. "You're too little!"

Papillon stuck her tongue out at me. "So are you!"

"Shut up, big brother," said Aurore, putting her hands on her hips. The train went over a switch and rattled heavily.

Suddenly, I heard a cry. It was Yves! He was halfway into the car. He wasn't tall enough to get in. His hands were grabbing uselessly for something to hold onto, but he was slipping backwards. The ground was starting to rush by.

"If he falls, the wheels'll cut his legs off!" gasped Aurore.

There was nothing to do. I dived forward, reached out the door, and tried to grab his belt. I missed his belt, but felt something and grabbed on. I don't know how I got the strength, but in one yank I pulled him aboard.

He rolled into the car, squirming and whining.

"He's hurt!" gasped Papillon.

Then Yves jumped onto his feet and punched me on the arm. Hard. His eyebrows were crossed in anger. He began fidgeting with his pants.

Aurore gave him a hug like she always did. "What is it, best buddy?" That was the pet name she used for him whenever they were mad at me.

Yves looked at me reproachfully and turned around to show how his underwear had been pulled up out of his pants. "Kip just gave me the worst skivvy-yank of my life."

Chapter 20

Chloroform!

"We've got to warn Colonel Steele!"

—From my journal
September 28, 1903

The train was soon clattering at top speed out of Whitehorse towards Bennett. Now that we were going too fast to jump off, having jumped on didn't seem like such a great idea.

Yves summed it up nicely. "Kip, Maman is going to kill you when she finds out you took us all to Skagway instead of school."

I tried the door to the passenger cars. "And it won't do Colonel Steele much good having us locked in the baggage car, either," I said. The side door was still wide open, but all the other doors were locked.

The lock on the door was a good one and the hinges were solidly built. I couldn't see anyway of getting through the door.

"We could scream and shout," I suggested.

"No. The conductor would catch us and put us off the train at the next stop," said Aurore. "Who wants to get off in Robinson or Carcross?"

We sat down on the luggage. Besides Captain von Neidling's suitcases and bags of rocks, there were also crates of butter, boxes of canned goods and bags of potatoes that they hadn't unloaded in

Whitehorse for some reason. There were even a couple of empty coffins stacked on the floor.

I sat on the bags of rocks. What was in them anyway? I pulled out my pocket knife and made a small cut in one of them. A few small pebbles tumbled out.

"Just rocks," I said.

"No," corrected Aurore. She was keen on geology and was always asking miners about rocks. "Look at the gold in it!"

"That's not gold," I said. "There's no dust or nuggets. It's not like any gold I've seen panned in the Yukon."

Above: A White Pass & Yukon Route train. Note the baggage car, perhaps the one that Kip, Aurore, Papillon and Yves rode in while trying to warn Colonel Steele. On that trip, the baggage car was the last car in the train not the first. (Photo courtesy of MacBride Museum 1999-251-273)

Aurore looked at me. "That's exactly right. That's because it's not placer gold, so you don't pan it. It's hard rock gold.[1]"

"But why would he be shipping rock like that to Skagway? Wouldn't you get the gold out and melt it into bars first?"

Aurore nodded. We continued to sit and think about this. We had lots of time.

Next was the luggage. Rudi's was unlocked. There was nothing interesting, although I did take the conductor's needle and thread and sew one of Rudi's pant legs shut.

I've always loved that joke. You have to do it to the right pant leg since most people put their left pant leg on first. They get the first leg on, then their foot won't fit through the second one and then they fall over. It's a classic.

Anyway, then we looked in Black Moran's bag. It had some socks, a shirt that was even dirtier than the one he was wearing and two Bibles. Then, underneath, Aurore found something.

"Guns!" she said. There were two pistol belts. One was like a cowboy's. It was greasy and worn. It was obviously Black Moran's. The other was shiny black leather with a strange belt. The buckle had German writing on it but the gun said "Colt" on the side.

It had to be the one I'd heard Rudi bragging about. "Captain von Neidling's new gun!" I gasped.

Papillon had a good suggestion. "I don't think they really need all those bullets!" she giggled. I knew how to use a rifle, of course, but Dad never let us touch handguns. Making sure they weren't pointing at anyone, I fiddled with the guns until I got the bullets out. Then Papillon threw them out the door into the forest. We put the guns back in the bags and closed them.

Captain von Neidling's sword was sitting on his suitcase. We pulled it out. It had a golden handle. The blade had something about Kaiser Wilhelm engraved in the shiny metal. They don't use swords in the Navy anymore and I knew it was supposed to be just

---

1.   Editor's Note: These Yukon children appear to have been well versed in mining. *Hard rock gold* is embedded in rock. This rock is blasted from pits and underground. Then it is crushed, extracted by grinding or dissolved with chemicals, and finally purified into gold bricks or bars. In contrast, *placer gold* has already been eroded from the rock. It is found in creek and river bottoms as nuggets, flakes or gold dust. The gold is loose and collected by pan, sluice box or dredge, all of which use water to wash away the less dense sand and gravel.

for wearing with his uniform on special occasions. But it was still kind of scary. We put it away.

Finally, we dragged out Captain von Neidling's suitcase. It had a big lock on the front. I tried to unscrew the hinges on the back, but they were riveted on.

"I can't get in!" I said. "What if there's another gun?"

"I know how to solve that problem!" said Papillon.

"What? Can you pick locks?" I asked sceptically.

"Don't need to. I've got a better idea!" She dragged Captain von Neidling's suitcase across the floor on its little wheels. Then she rolled it right out of the car! "Whoopsie!" she said. The suitcase arched through the air before smashing on a stump and spraying underwear and papers everywhere.

"Now that's creative thinking!" I said.

A few minutes later the train slowed down and rolled into Carcross. We looked out the door at the general store. Louie was standing right there with his father! I waved and he started to walk towards us.

Then I realized! If Louie could see us, then so could the conductor. I put my fingers over my lips and jumped behind the luggage. "Hide everybody!" I hissed.

Louie understood. "Excuse me, Mr. Conductor, sir," he said suddenly as the conductor came into sight.

Fortunately the conductor's back was to us since he was looking at Louie. "What is it?" he snapped.

"Err," stammered Louie. I could see he was staring into our car. Papillon's feet were showing! I grabbed her ankles and pulled them out of sight as Louie finally opened his mouth. "Err, is that train going to Bennett?"

I almost laughed. I'd have to give a Louie a hard time for not being able to think up a better question than that! It worked though.

The conductor turned back towards him. "Of course!" he said in annoyance. "That's where the tracks go!" He turned his back on Louie and tossed another suitcase into our car.

"Have a good trip!" shouted Louie. I could tell he meant it for us.

The conductor just rolled his eyes. "Stupid kids," he muttered to himself. Then he slammed the side door shut.

We were completely locked in!

The train slowly picked up speed. I looked out the back window and saw Louie running behind us. I waved. He gave me a thumbs up and slowly disappeared out of sight as we got to full speed.

It seemed to take forever as the train wound its way along Lake Bennett towards Bennett Station. I figured they would have to let us out there. Our car was the last one on the train, though, and we had a great view of the lake out of the window in the back door.

It was pretty boring. Not much of an adventure at all. I couldn't help thinking about Colonel Steele and hoping he was all right. But Yves just lay down in one of the coffins and had a nap. At least until Aurore said it was too creepy and made him sleep on the floor.

Finally, as we slowed down near Bennett, we heard a key slide into the lock. I was about to shout with joy, but suddenly something told me we should hide.

"Quick! Behind the luggage everybody! Just in case!" We scrambled behind the potatoes and bags of rocks and lay still. The conductor came in, followed by another man. I glimpsed between two suitcases. He had a black hat … a black jacket … a black beard … it was Black Moran!

"So," drawled Black Moran. He spit some tobacco juice onto the luggage just in front of me. "You got space for 'em back here?"

"I guess so," said the conductor in a quiet voice. He seemed nervous. He kept looking back and forth between Black Moran's priest costume and the long rope Black Moran held in his left hand.

"Good," said Black Moran. "We're getting pretty sick playing nicey-nice up there with Sam Steele and his stupid pal. Next thing, they'll offer me a cup of tea."

The conductor turned towards Black Moran. He looked quite pale. "Umm ... Are you, um, sure you want to do this? Sam Steele's pretty famous."

Black Moran snarled. "Vengeance is mine, sayeth the Lord." Then he laughed and kicked one of the coffins. "Perfect. We'll stow famous Sam Steele and his stupid English sidekick in these!"

The conductor looked at Black Moran. He was terrified. He took off his hat and wiped the sweat off his brow even though it was pretty cold in the baggage car. Black Moran grabbed the conductor by the shirt. "If you're not careful, Mr. Conductor sir, we'll be needing *three* coffins!" Black Moran put his arm around the conductor and hugged him in a way the conductor didn't seem to find very reassuring. "Just remember. If you help us get to Skagway and keep your mouth shut, you'll get plenty of gold. Do anything else, and you'll just get lead!"

Black Moran laughed, grabbed his bag and took out his pistol belt. "We're close enough to Alaska for me to wear this, I figure!" Then he grabbed Captain von Neidling's pistol and slipped it into his pocket.

Just then, the train whistle hooted and we began to slow down for Bennett. Aurore and I exchanged glances behind the potato sacks. "We've got to warn Colonel Steele!" she whispered.

But before I could move, Black Moran grabbed the door handle. He held the door open for the conductor as the train wheels screeched to a halt in front of Bennett Station. I didn't hear the conductor lock the door.

Once they were gone, I jumped up. I watched through the window as they disappeared into the car ahead of us. Quietly, I opened the door and slipped across the little walkway onto the platform of the car ahead of us.

I looked in the window of the door, then swung it open to shout to Colonel Steele. But what I saw froze me instead. Colonel Steele was sitting at the far end of the car, facing away from me and reading the paper. Meanwhile, Black Moran and two men were sneaking up the aisle towards him.

It must have taken a split second, but it seemed like an hour. I tried to shout but nothing came out.

Just then, I saw Colonel Steele's face in the mirror at the far end of the car. He was watching Black Moran creep down the aisle! Colonel Steele bent down as if tying his shoe, then suddenly grabbed his suitcase from the floor in front of him. In one quick motion, he stood, turned and threw it right into Black Moran's stomach!

Black Moran fell backwards and knocked over his henchmen.

Meanwhile Colonel Steele jumped up and ran for the door at the other end of the car.

"He's going to make it!" I thought.

But then, to my horror, the bathroom door flew open across the corridor. Colonel Steele hurtled into it at full speed then went sprawling all over the floor.

Percy stepped out of the bathroom while adjusting his belt. He looked down at Colonel Steele on the floor. "I say, Steele! Don't you colonials knock?"

In an instant, Black Moran and his gang were on top of Colonel Steele.

That's when I realized I should make a run for it. I turned to escape, but I suddenly found myself face to face with Captain von Neidling!

I tried to duck under his arms and squeeze out the door, but his arm flashed forward and I felt his hand grip my collar. "Impudent rascal!" he hissed in my ear. He pulled me onto the little platform on the back of Colonel Steele's car.

He held me in the air and stared into my face. His lips twisted into a devilish smile under the admiral's hat. My feet weren't even touching the ground. I could feel my collar tighten around my throat as his grip stiffened. It was getting hard to breathe! He watched me turn red. I saw the points on his teeth glint in the sunlight as his smile broadened.

A few seconds later, Black Moran appeared in the doorway. "Did this one get away from you, Moran?" said Captain von Neidling mockingly. "What do you think we should do with him now?"

As I dangled, Black Moran leaned back, fingered his pistol, and thought. "He'll fit in the coffin with the scrawny Limey. We can figure out what to do with them later."

The coffin! I squirmed to get away but it was useless.

Over Captain von Neidling's shoulder I could see Black Moran's gang pushing Colonel Steele and Percy towards us. Their hands were tied behind their backs.

Black Moran drew his gun. "Nice to see you again, Colonel! Hands up!" Then he laughed. "I forgot. You're tied up!"

I knew Black Moran's gun wasn't loaded. I opened my mouth. "It's not—" But before I could say anything, Captain von Neidling gave my collar a quick twist.

"Well, there's one more of you than planned," said Captain von Neidling with a laugh. He hoisted me higher. "But the Yukon is the land of Pioneer Spirit. We'll find a solution!"

"You'd better release us before you get in even more trouble, von Neidling," said Colonel Steele. He was calm. Amazingly calm for a man tied up with a gun pointed at him.

In fact, he was so calm it seemed to make Captain von Neidling angry. "You British are so smug," he snarled. "You think you are entitled to an empire but Germany isn't!"

Colonel Steele smiled. "I think we're safe. Last time I checked, the German Army couldn't walk on water."

"Don't forget the German Navy! We will soon be stronger than you. And we'll make sure you can't run to your American friends for reinforcements."

"Your scheme will never work," said Colonel Steele. I wondered if Colonel Steele knew what Captain von Neidling's scheme even was.

But this didn't stop Captain von Neidling. "You don't even know what my scheme is," he shouted. "And I might as well tell you since you can't do a thing about it now! Operation Aeolus can't fail. Once we announce we've found the mother lode of Klondike gold—a second Gold Rush!—at Bennett, there's no way President Roosevelt will be able to agree to a peaceful settlement of the Alaska-Canada border dispute. The negotiations in London will be ruined! Especially since half the U.S. Senate owns shares in Star Mine!" Captain von Neidling was talking faster and faster. Spit was flying from his lips and a wild look filled his eyes. "Once we tell the newspapers, there's no way anyone will be able to calm things down."

"So that's why you've called it Aeolus. Once the bag of wind is opened, no one can stop the storm. And I suppose *you* are Boreas," said Colonel Steele mockingly. "von Neidling ... not just a wind bag, but Boreas the mighty North Wind himself!

"Shut up Steele!"

"Come on, von Neidling. It'll never work. Everyone knows you haven't found gold at the Star Mine! No one will believe you!"

"Well, I *have* found gold. I bought it from a mine in Dawson City. But it's all now in burlap sacks marked 'Star Mine' in the baggage car of this train," said Captain von Neidling.

He laughed. "When I show the American newspapers in Skagway, it'll be like the Klondike Gold Rush has started again. It'll be front page news in every city in the United States. Plus how two idiotic British secret agents—and a boy—tried to steal the gold!" Captain von Neidling's eyes were getting even wilder.

"But why?" stuttered Percy, looking bewildered.

Captain von Neidling looked at Percy and snorted. "After my Operation Aeolus, Britain and America will be enemies. America will never back Britain against Germany." He shook his fist in the air. "There's no way Britain will be able to stop Germany in Africa! In Europe! Anywhere!"

Colonel Steele suddenly looked worried. But just for a second. "And I suppose the main point is to make Kaiser Wilhelm think you are a hero instead of a failed mine owner," he said in an unimpressed voice.

The train whistle blew before Captain von Neidling could reply. We heard the engine starting to move.

"Is Doctor Moran ready to operate?" asked Captain von Neidling, laughing shrilly at Black Moran.

"Yes, sir." Black Moran nodded at the two men behind Colonel Steele. One grabbed Colonel Steele's arms and, before he could move, the other clamped a cloth over Colonel Steele's mouth.

"Chloroform!" exclaimed Percy as Colonel Steele slumped to the floor.

"Exactly. He'll sleep like a baby," said Black Moran. "Your turn!" The man with the cloth poured some more chloroform out of a can onto the cloth and moved towards Percy.

"Oooohhh—" sighed Percy. He fainted before the cloth even got near him.

Chapter 21

Chase at the Top of the World

"Alaska Panic: Word that President Plans more Troops for Alaska if U.S. Loses in London"

—Newspaper clipping from Mr. Taylor
September 28, 1903

Captain von Neidling and his gang laughed as Percy slumped to the floor. "Two for the price of one!" exclaimed Black Moran.

Black Moran opened his pocket, pulled out Captain von Neidling's new pistol and gave it to him. Out of the corner of my eye, I could see Captain von Neidling put the pistol in his pocket and then put his left hand on the iron railing around the platform. His right hand seemed to be gripping my throat tighter every second. "And finally, your turn!" he said.

Then I saw the safety railing. It was a heavy iron bar the conductor would put down across the walkway when passengers wanted to stand on the platform and look at the mountains. As Captain von Neidling and Black Moran joked about putting me in a coffin, I slowly moved my hand up the wall and unclipped the safety bar.

Then—as hard as I could—I rammed it down on Captain von Neidling's left hand!

He screamed and dropped me. I leaped over the side of the train.

"Get him!" hissed Captain von Neidling. He pulled out his pistol and waved it at Black Moran, who leaped off the train too. I started to run towards the engine to get the engineer's attention, but suddenly Rudi jumped off the front of the car and ran towards me.

I turned around and ran back towards where I'd come from. Captain von Neidling jumped down off the platform right in front of me! He grimaced and stretched out his long arms.

I saw that there was another train engine on the track beside ours, so I dodged around the other side of it and kept on running. Suddenly, I sensed a shadow above me. Captain von Neidling had jumped into the engineer's cab! His arm flashed out of the engineer's window towards me. "Gotcha!" he cried in triumph.

But I ducked and his fist closed on nothing but air.

I looked back to see him pull out his gun. "No!" I cried.

But nothing happened.

I looked back to see him silhouetted against the blue sky, waving his pistol and stamping his feet. "Moran, where are my bullets!" he shrieked. He took off his fancy navy hat and threw it on the ground.

"I'll get him," shouted Black Moran. He was still dressed like a priest. He jumped off our train and ran at me, his white priest's collar flapping wildly. Then he dived at my feet like a football tackle.

"Jump!" said a voice in my head. So I jumped! I looked down to see my boots flying through the air. I can remember the picture perfectly. Everything slowed down. I saw Black Moran's beard, blood-shot eyes and white collar. I felt his fingertips brush the bottoms of my boots for a second. Then I flew over him and he hit the ground with a huge "oomph."

I took off like it was the school track meet with Dawson City Elementary and didn't look back.

"Devil's spawn!" shouted Black Moran.

"Shut up and get him!" retorted Captain von Neidling. In an instant, Black Moran was up and after me.

Over my shoulder, I could see the train starting to move.

"Help!" I called to the engineer, but I was drowned out by the engine's whistle.

"I'll get you this time," gasped Black Moran. He was gaining, but I guess he was too tired to throw in a Bible quote.

I faked left, then made a sudden dodge to the right—it's my favourite hockey move—and headed for Bennett Station. I burst into the great hall through the end doors. The room was full of train passengers having their Yukon baked beans lunch before heading back to Skagway on the other train.

"Captain von Neidling is going to kidnap Sam Steele!" I shouted.

"Pardon me, boy?" said one old man.

"Did he say Sam Steele?" said another lady.

"Maybe it's some kind of Klondike re-enactment they're putting on for us," said another.

Black Moran suddenly appeared in the doorway of the station behind me. He was panting and looking angrier than a grizzly that's lost his salmon. He lunged at me. With people on all sides, I jumped up onto the table. A plate of beans clattered onto the floor.

"Why, he's dressed like a priest!" said one old lady.

"Realistic!" said the old man enthusiastically.

"Captain von Neidling is going to kidnap ..." My words trailed off as they looked up at me in expectation. "Oh, never mind!" I turned. The tables were in long straight rows with plates of beans, pitchers of water and baskets of fresh bread. I jumped over the first bread basket and took off across the room jumping from table to table.

Black Moran was after me in a second. Everyone cheered and clapped. Black Moran was gaining on me. Then he made a mistake. Instead of stepping in the middle of the table behind me, he made an extra long step and reached the edge of the table I was just running across.

Unfortunately (for him), the end of a table isn't a smart place to stand. I felt my end rise up in the air as I was jumping off it. Looking back, I saw him hit the floor as all the hot beans, coffee and cookies flew into the air.

I raced out the other door. Where to run to now? To Carcross? Into the bush? Black Moran burst out of the station. He was covered in beans but it didn't seem to slow him down.

Down the tracks, the train was beginning to pick up speed. I turned to chase it. "I've … got … to … warn … Aurore," I thought as I ran.

I finally caught up to the train just as it was really beginning to accelerate. I grabbed the back railing and pulled myself up onto the platform. Black Moran was still a hundred feet away. I could see his lips moving with shouts and Bible quotes, but the engine drowned him out.

I peeked into the baggage car just in time to see Captain von Neidling nailing the top on the second coffin. Percy and Colonel Steele were inside! Behind Captain von Neidling, I could see Yves's foot sticking out from behind a suitcase. My brother and sisters were still trapped in there. I looked back down the tracks. The driver wasn't going very fast at all, probably because the tracks were being repaired. Black Moran was still running after us.

Things were pretty grim all right.

Finally we sped up a bit, forcing Black Moran to pull up and stop running. Inside the baggage car, the hammering stopped and I heard a door slam. Captain von Neidling had finished his nasty job and had returned to the comfy chairs in the passenger car. I snuck back into the baggage car, checking for any guards. The side door was still open and the two coffins were stacked in the middle of the floor.

I quickly told Aurore, Papillon and Yves about Captain von Neidling's crazy plan.

But just as I finished, the door burst open. It was Rudi, still dressed in his admiral's outfit!

"I knew you were back on the train, frog!" he laughed.

But he had miscalculated something. I wasn't at school, under strict instructions from Dad, Maman, Mr. Galpin and every adult in the Yukon to control my temper! I lunged towards him.

He jumped easily out of the way and I barged past him.

He laughed. "You'll have to do better than that, Kip!"

I smiled grimly at him. "I wasn't aiming for *you*!" He looked slightly puzzled so I continued. "I just wanted to close this door so you couldn't get away." I pushed the carriage door closed and twisted the lock. A look of worry flashed across his face. He wasn't used to me standing up to him.

"Get him, Kip!" shouted Yves. I dived at Rudi. I grabbed his costume jacket. We swayed back and forth. I tried to push him towards the open door as the ground whizzed by.

"You're crazy!" he shouted in alarm. With a surprising burst of strength, he pushed me back over the coffins and ran for the door. Before he could unlock it, I was on him.

Yves and Papillon screamed. "Go Kip!"

Rudi pushed me off again. Then he grabbed his father's sword off the luggage pile. He pulled out the blade. It gleamed in the Yukon sun. "You're in for it now, frog!" he said. His bully voice was back.

I gulped. With the sword, he looked almost like a real naval officer.

"Watch out!" shouted Aurore as Rudi swung wildly at me. I dodged and rolled to the corner of the car. The old hockey stick the conductor used to open the upper windows was there. I grabbed it and swung back.

He parried my blow. The sword sunk deep into my stick. I swung again, but he ducked and all I got was his admiral's hat. He jumped back as his hat bounced out the open door and disappeared onto the tracks.

"Get rid of the gold!" I shouted to Aurore. "He needs it to prove his mine has gold!" She couldn't lift the first bag, but she snipped the string on top and dumped it out. Papillon and Yves started throwing the rocks out the door.

"Stop that!" shouted Rudi. He moved towards Aurore, but I raised my stick and he backed off. Swish! He swung at me again but missed. Swish! Whack! Swish! I swung furiously at him to drive him away from Papillon and Yves.

I glanced back as Aurore dumped another bag onto the floor. Suddenly, Rudi threw the conductor's tea cup at me. It hit me in the face. Rudi leaped over the coffins and kicked Yves backwards. He fell back hard against the wall. I jumped up on the coffins and swung. Rudi went for my feet but I jumped.

He swung so hard that when he missed, his arms went all the way around like a baseball batter. Before he could recover, I brought my stick down on his face. It glanced off his nose and hit his shoulder.

He cried out in pain. I swung again, but he managed to get his sword in the way.

Aurore dumped out a third bag and a fourth as we circled each other. Rudi tried to drive Aurore or Papillon away as they furiously threw the gold rocks out the side door and I tried to stand in his way.

Suddenly Yves shouted. "It's Black Moran! He's on a bike!"

"That's impossible!" I shouted. Then I looked through the open back door. Sure enough, there was Black Moran rattling along the rails behind us. My heart sank. He was on a velocipede![1] His legs were pumping furiously on the pedals. The train still wasn't going very fast and he was catching up!

Black Moran was waving his arms angrily at us. Unlike a bicycle, you don't have to steer a velocipede.

"When he catches up, you're history!" gloated Rudi. I swung for him again, but I was getting tired. He easily parried my blow. I watched nervously as the train slowed around a bend and Black

---

1.   Editor's Note: Velocipedes were a kind of rail-bicycle used by railway workers to travel between jobs on the tracks when no trains were available. See photo at end of this chapter.

Moran got closer. He was close enough that I could see the frenzy in his eyes.

Then Papillon—bless her!—had an idea. She even said it in French so Rudi couldn't understand it. "Aurore et Yves! Jetez les pierres à Black Moran!"

It was brilliant. Black Moran had to keep pedalling so there was no way he could dodge the rocks. But first I had to get Rudi out of the way.

I made a furious attack on Rudi's left, hoping he would dodge right. That way I could get behind him and make him trade places with me.

But it didn't work. He knew I was trying something and wouldn't budge. I could see Black Moran getting closer.

Then Aurore had an idea. In English, she pretended to be mad at me and exclaimed, "Kip, just leave him and go uncouple this car from the passenger car!"

This made Rudi move! "No way!" he shouted. With a flurry of sword swings he ran past me to guard the door to the passenger car.

"Merci!" shouted Papillon. She grabbed a nasty looking rock the size of a baseball and ran out on the back platform and threw it at Black Moran.

It missed him. "Ha!" he laughed. "David needed a sling to stop Goliath!" He pedalled even faster.

Then Papillon threw another. He tried to dodge it, but it hit him in the leg and he missed a stroke on his pedals. "Ow!" he shouted, plus a few words that aren't in the Bible.

Then Papillon hit him in the arm.

Enraged, he pulled out his pistol and pointed it at us. Papillon and Yves dived for cover. But nothing happened. He didn't have any bullets!

Yves jumped up. "Fire!" he shouted. He began to throw small rocks furiously. They mostly missed, but Black Moran had to dodge a few. Another hit him in the leg and he missed another stroke on the pedals.

Aurore had a good arm too. She was throwing egg-sized chunks of gold rock. Hard and fast.

But then we passed the summit. It was downhill from here on. Black Moran started gaining. Fast. Now his problem was that the closer he got, the easier it got for Aurore, Papillon and Yves to hit him. But eventually the engineer would put on the brakes and the velocipede would run into the back of our train and be able to jump aboard.

"Throw faster!" I shouted. Aurore opened another bag of gold rocks.

It was Papillon that ended it. She ran out of rocks and ran back into the car. As Aurore and Yves continued to throw, she ran back towards the door as fast as she could. Her arm cocked back and she threw. I watched as a can of Pacific condensed milk from the conductor's desk arced through the doorway and connected with Black Moran's nose.

He toppled backwards off the velocipede and disappeared. The girls and Yves cheered as the velocipede continued to coast down-hill towards us without a rider.

Rudi was really worried now. He launched a new attack, breaking the end off my hockey stick. We circled the coffins as we swung and jabbed at each other. It was getting really scary now. We were on the Alaska side. Sometimes we were on bridges with nothing below us for 1000 feet. Other times, the door was zipping past straight rock faces.

Suddenly, we were in a tunnel. It was pitch black. I ducked just in time to hear the sword swish over my head. I jabbed and felt my hockey stick hit something soft. Rudi gasped. The light reappeared to reveal Rudi holding his stomach and looking madder than ever.

We were both exhausted, but kept circling. The floor was starting to get slippery from the waterfall spray splashing in.

Would it never stop, I wondered? Then I noticed Yves had stopped pushing the rocks out the door. Instead, he crawled quietly in front of the open door.

He was right behind Rudi.

I suddenly realized what he was doing. Have you ever had a friend crawl up behind someone on the playground so the person falls backwards when you push them? I have. In fact, Mr. Galpin gave me the strap for it.

Yves braced himself. I manoeuvred back and forth until Rudi was just in the right place.

Then I lunged.

Rudi tried to take a step back. He didn't know Yves was there. Suddenly Rudi was teetering backwards by the door. I gave him a quick poke in the chest with the butt end of my hockey stick and over he went!

Yves and I jumped to the edge. Were we on a 1000 foot high bridge? Fortunately, we saw Rudi land on a pile of railway gravel and skid into a mossy bank. I noticed we were almost in Skagway.

"He was lucky," said Yves.

"Black Moran must have been praying for him," I said.

Above: Yukon pioneer Paul Cyr riding a White Pass & Yukon Route velocipede similar to the one used by Black Moran. (Photo courtesy of Paul Cyr)

Chapter 22

Yukon Gold ... Potatoes

===============

"Alaska: Final Decision Scheduled for October 12"

—*Newspaper clipping from Mr. Taylor*
September 27, 1903

After I pushed Rudi out of the train car, we dumped the rest of the rocks over the side as fast as we could. It felt kind of funny throwing gold out the door.

"Disconnect the car, Kip!" said Aurore when we were done.

"I don't know how!" I said. "Those couplings are huge!"

Then I had a better idea. In fact, I don't know if I'll ever have another idea this good. "Quick! Clean up the car!" I opened a box of groceries, grabbed the empty burlap sacks and started to restuff them furiously so they looked full.

The train was slowing as we entered the long straight stretch before Skagway. "We're almost in Skagway! Hurry!"

We were about to jump off, when Yves heard a noise from inside one of the coffins. "We almost forgot Colonel Steele!" he exclaimed. I looked around quickly for a hammer to open the coffins, but Papil-lon had thrown all the tools at Black Moran.

"Oh well," I said. "At least they're in coffins and this'll hurt less than it hurt Rudi." And I pushed Percy's coffin off the side.

Colonel Steele's was a lot heavier, but eventually all four of us got it over the side too.

Then it was our turn. Grabbing my favourite hockey stick, we waited until the train slowed near the old cemetery.

"Jump!" I shouted. We landed in a heap. I scraped my knees. Yves ripped his pants.

We rolled into the bushes as the train rolled away. We were right in front of Frank Reid's grave.[1]

We ran back up the track to find Colonel Steele's coffin. I grabbed a rusty railway spike and started working the top off. Once there was a little gap, I shoved in my hockey stick and pried it all the way open.

Colonel Steele moaned and sat up. He looked dazed and pale like a ghost. "Papillon," I said. "You can tell Mary at the Golden North that I believe in the dead rising from their graves."

Colonel Steele blinked and looked around. It took a minute for his eyes to focus on us. He cleared his throat and started to speak. "You know the rules. You need at least 2000 pounds of supplies to enter Canada."[2] Then he put his head back down and went back to sleep.

We got Percy's coffin open too, but couldn't wake him either.

While the others took care of Colonel Steele, I decided to run into town and see what would happen when the train got there.

The train tracks went down Broadway Street to the centre of Skagway. I didn't want Captain von Neidling to see me, so I ran

---

1.   Editor's Note: The Skagway Cemetery is about one mile from downtown Skagway. As recounted in Aurore of the Yukon, Frank Reid was the Skagway hero (and friend of Aurore and Yves) who defended the town against notorious frontier gunman Soapy Smith. He died in the famous shoot out on July 8th, 1898 after killing Soapy and was buried on the edge of town.

2.   Editor's Note: Colonel Steele's chloroform-induced hallucination appears to have taken him back to 1898, when he required everyone entering the Yukon to have a full year's worth of supplies.

across to State Street. Halfway there, I saw a bicycle laying on a lawn. The Law of the Yukon says you can borrow something if you really need it and you bring it back in one piece. So I grabbed the bike and took off towards the train station.

As I got near the station, I heard a huge cheer go up. The train was just arriving and there was a huge crowd. He must have sent word that something big was happening. Captain von Neidling was standing on the passenger car platform. He was back in normal clothes. He waved to the crowd. It was exactly where he had been holding me by the neck just a few minutes before.

The engine whistled. People cheered. Newspaper cameras went pop.

Captain von Neidling raised his arms. Everyone was quiet.

"Everyone! This is a historic moment. You'll be able to tell your kids you were there when the second Klondike Gold Rush started!" There was a huge cheer.

"In this baggage car is the proof. Just like on June 24th, 1897 when the S.S. Excellent docked in Seattle with a million dollars of gold[3], this gold will set off a Yukon Gold Rush like no one has ever seen before."

The crowd cheered some more. He raised his hands. "I'd like to give my son Rudi the honour …" He paused. "Rudi? Rudi?" he called. I'm afraid I smirked as one of his gang went to look for Rudi. "Anyway, I will now unveil the Yukon Gold you've all been waiting for."

He lifted the safety bar I had slammed on his hand (he grimaced slightly, I thought) and walked across to the baggage car. He opened the door and stepped in. He looked slightly surprised to find the side door already open. Whether he noticed the coffins were gone, I have no idea.

The crowd was silent as he walked up to the pile of burlap sacks. He reached into his pocket, pulled out a pocket knife and slit open

---

3.   Editor's Note: Actually it was the S.S. Excelsior on July 14th, 1898, in San Francisco, and it was $500,000 worth of gold.

the top sack. Then he shouted "Yukon Gold" and dumped the sack onto the floor.

There was total silence as potatoes cascaded onto the floor and bounced out the door into the crowd.

Captain von Neidling was stunned. He grabbed another sack and slashed it open. More potatoes, just as we had re-stuffed the sacks.

"Yeah, Yukon Gold potatoes!"[4] shouted a man scornfully from the crowd. Laughter erupted. People began to pick up the potatoes from the ground and throw them at Captain von Neidling. He stood there, completely speechless, until one of his henchman quietly slid the side door of the baggage car shut.

---

4.   Editor's Note: According to official sources, the Yukon Gold potato was developed by the Canadian Department of Agriculture and the University of Guelph and released in 1980 well after the events described in Kip's story. However, historians cannot exclude the possibility that the name of this early maturing cultivar, particularly well suited to baking, soup and potato salad, was inspired by von Neidling's plot.

Epilogue

"We feel sure that when the first flush of natural displeasure has passed away, Canadians will see that a definite settlement, however unpalatable and even harsh in its bearing on their interests, is infinitely preferable to a continuance of the harassing uncertainty."

—*London Standard*
October 23, 1903

"The President and the Cabinet regard the award as far and away the greatest diplomatic success which the United States have gained for a generation."

—*Washington Post*
October 21, 1903

"The feeling of indignation in Vancouver over the Alaskan award is so intense that prominent citizens openly give voice to sentiments hostile to England."

—*Victoria Colonist*
October 24, 1903

Colonel Steele and Percy woke up groggy and with bruises they couldn't explain. In fact, it took several days for Colonel Steele to realize that the only way he could have gotten off the train was being pushed off in his coffin.

Despite Aurore's suggestion that we go immediately to the American police and tell them everything, both Colonel Steele and Percy refused. "It could cause a diplomatic incident," said Percy. "Too darn embarrassing," said Colonel Steele.

Instead, we quietly got the next train back to Canada. When we got to Bennett and stopped for our White Pass and Yukon Route lunch of baked beans, Black Moran was sitting quietly in the corner with a bandage on his head reading his Bible.

I suggested to Colonel Steele that Black Moran should be arrested. "It could cause a diplomatic incident," said Percy. "Too darn embarrassing," said Colonel Steele.

When we returned to Whitehorse, Maman and Dad were waiting at the station with our dog D'Artagnan. Colonel Steele had sent a telegram. We could see them as the train rolled in.

"If she waves, we're grounded for a year," said Aurore.

"And if she doesn't, it's forever," said Yves.

Colonel Steele gulped as the train stopped. D'Artagnan barked and bounded towards the train. Maman didn't move a muscle.

Colonel Steele got off first. He tried to say something, but Maman interrupted him.

"Monsieur le Colonel! Ça ne m'est rien s'ils ont sauvé l'Empire Britannique, ils seront en penitence pour 100 ans!"

Yves was horrified. "Grounded until 2003! Will hockey even still exist?"

We trudged home. Slowly, since even with his cane Dad could barely walk.

Percy went back to London and Colonel Steele went back to South Africa. Before he left, he made us promise never to tell what had happened. "Sometimes, you just have to be satisfied that you did the right thing even if no one else knows it," he said. He muttered something else too. Something like, "Plus, it would ruin Percy's career in London," whatever that meant.

Slowly life got back to normal. I was only released from grounding in order to work at the Telegraph Office or the hotel. Aurore went back to work at Taylor and Drury's after school. Papillon babysat and Yves delivered bread for Maman in his wagon.

But I could do the math. We would never earn enough to take Dad to Vancouver for his operation.

As for Dad, he tried hard to stop us from worrying about him. But we could tell he was sad. Not only was his leg really painful, but he couldn't do the things he loved any more. No horse riding. No rigging up the teams to go wood cutting. He hadn't run a boat through Miles Canyon once the whole summer! I would almost cry when I saw him hobbling down Main Street to have another meeting with the Bank Manager.

On October 21st we heard the news from London. The Alaska Boundary Tribunal had made its decision. President Roosevelt's three friends and the British member had outvoted the two Canadian members. Everyone in Canada was bitterly disappointed.

"I don't understand why everyone's so upset," I said. "The border stays more or less where it was. Bennett is still in Canada. Skagway's still in America."

Aurore agreed. "And there's been no war. Canada, America and Britain are still friends ... mostly!" She thought about it for a minute. "I guess most Canadians thought they deserved Skagway. They're probably most upset because they feel bullied by President Roosevelt."

"And let down by the British!"

"It's funny," said Aurore. "All those angry writers in the newspapers seem to have forgotten that there could have been a war."

Then, one day in December after school, there was a knock on the door. It was Mr. Congden, the Commissioner of the Yukon Territory!

Mr. Congden had to sit by himself in the living room for a long time while Maman combed our hair, made me find socks without holes and so on.

"Well, Mr. and Mrs. Dutoit," he said, once we had finally all found places to sit in the living room and he had had a sip of his tea. "This world just keeps getting stranger and stranger. The bag from Ottawa came in today. There were two things in it for you. Well, for the kids actually."

Maman looked sideways at us. I think she was trying to figure out what punishment would be even worse than getting grounded for 100 years.

Mr. Congden went on. "The first thing is—and I really don't under-stand this—is a thank you letter from President Roosevelt. Doesn't say for what. Just says that Sam Steele told Captain Richardson the whole story and that he thanks you and wants you to visit the White House next time you're in Washington." He paused and looked at us over his glasses. We didn't move a muscle. He went on. "Not only that, it includes a newspaper clipping from the Washington Post about Captain von Neidling inventing a new kind of potato called the Yukon Gold. First I've heard of it!" Mr. Congden shook his head in disbelief and gave us the letter.

"And the second item is even stranger, if you can believe it. It's a cheque from the Foreign Office in London. There's a strange letter from a fellow named Percy Brown too. Name seems to ring a bell. Wasn't there a fellow up here during the Gold Rush by that name? Called him the Piccadilly Dude if I recall. Anyway, the letter has a bunch of gibberish about paying someone called Agent Y1 for ser-vices rendered to the empire, honorarium payments, secret codes, don't tell anyone and all that."

He looked at my parents. Then at us. My parents looked puzzled. The rest of us managed to keep looking serious.

"Anyway," he said, "I also got a note from Sam Steele saying to ignore Percy and just give the money to Kip. He'd know what to do with it. At least that's what Sam Steele says. And Sam Steele is usu-ally right."

"How much is the cheque for, sir?" I asked.

"Quite a bit, Kip." Mr. Congden smiled. "I'd just say there ought to be enough for a trip to see the doctor in Vancouver."

Dad put his arm around me. "Kip, I don't know what you did ... but thanks!"

I looked up at him. "Aren't you mad at me? If I hadn't dropped those boxes you would never have been hurt!"

He looked at me and laughed. "That's the silliest thing I ever heard! Didn't you know that Mr. Liebherr quit Star Mine because he found out they were using unsafe old dynamite? You didn't make it blow. Didn't you know that?" He looked at me. I shook my head. Dad smiled. "First you get me to Dr. Nicholson's in record time, then you get the British Foreign Office to pay for my operation. I can only say one thing ..." He took my hand and shook it like a grown up. "Thank you, my friend!"

It was the best thing I've ever heard. I don't know why, but I started to cry.

THE ALASKA-CANADA BOUNDARY DISPUTE
BY KIP DUTOIT
MR. GALPIN'S CLASS, DECEMBER 12, 1903
LAMBERT STREET PUBLIC SCHOOL
WHITEHORSE, YUKON TERRITORY

The Alaska-Canada boundary dispute was a major international argument. It almost started a war. The United States was on one side and Canada and Britain were on the other. Canada claimed that Skagway was actually part of Canada. The U.S. claimed that Bennett was really in Alaska (see map).

The problem started almost 80 years ago in 1825. This was before the U.S. bought Alaska from the Russian Empire in 1867 for 2 cents an acre (pretty cheap!)[1]. At the time, the British ran Canada and the Russians owned Alaska. Hardly any British or Russian people lived there so you could really say that it was the native people that owned it. But no one asked them.

The British and Russians signed a treaty in 1825 describing where the border was between Alaska and the Yukon. The problem was that none of the diplomats who signed the treaty had ever been to Alaska! And their maps were not very good.

The Americans sent some surveyors to study the border in 1888. The Canadian government even sent a spy to follow them.[2] But the surveyors didn't fix the problem.

---

1.   Kip, we don't put slang comments in school essays. And although 2 cents an acre seems cheap now, at the time many Americans made fun of Mr. Seward for buying Alaska. $7 million was a lot of money in 1867 and people jokingly called Alaska names like "Seward's Folly," "Seward's Ice Box" or even "Seward's Polar Bear Garden."—Mr. Galpin

2.   Kip, we don't make things up in school essays! A Canadian spy! Ridiculous.—Mr. Galpin. (Editor's Note: Kip was actually correct, although how a schoolboy in Whitehorse would know this remains a mystery. According to Norman Penlington in The Alaska Boundary Dispute, the Canadian government did indeed send a man "incognito" to spy on the American surveyors.)

This didn't really matter until gold was discovered in 1896 in the Yukon and the Klondike Gold Rush started. Suddenly, it was very important to figure out where the border was. Canada wanted to own Skagway so that it could control who got into the Yukon so Canadian miners could get most of the gold. The U.S. wanted the same. Plus, no one knew where the next gold find might happen. Each country wanted to get as much land as possible.

So everyone had to dust off the old treaty! All the people who had written it were dead. There was plenty to argue about. First, the treaty was in French so each side had its own translation. The treaty said the border started at a place called the "Portland Channel," but no one knew exactly where that was! And it said the border should follow the mountains, but which mountains? And when it said "coast," did it mean just the ocean coast or also the coast of inlets like the one Skagway is on?

These sound like silly things to argue about, but there were millions of dollars and—even worse—national pride at stake.

In 1898, Canada sent Colonel[3] Sam Steele to Skagway to establish the border. He thought about declaring that Skagway was in Canada and setting up there. But there were thousands of Americans already in Skagway who didn't think they were in Canada! So he decided to set up a temporary border at the summit of the Chilkoot Pass. The American commander in Dyea, Alaska, meanwhile, tried to order Steele to move further inland. He thought the Chilkoot was 100% U.S. territory. Steele refused. He put up the British flag, plus a machine gun to make his point. People settled down to use the temporary border while they waited for U.S. President Roosevelt, Prime Minister Laurier of Canada and the British to settle the problem.

---

3.   Kip, at the time he was just a North West Mounted Police Superintendent and not yet the world-famous "Klondike Law Man" who kept Soapy Smith's gang out of the Yukon.—Mr. Galpin

Above: Newspaper clipping with map of the Alaska Boundary Dispute.
(Courtesy of the Perry-Castañeda Library Map Collection at the
University of Texas at Austin)

Finally, in 1903 everyone agreed to appoint six experts to solve the problem. They were called the Alaska Boundary Tribunal and they were supposed to be fair to all sides. Three were American, two were Canadian and one was British. The British member was Lord Alverstone, a famous British judge with a reputation for honesty.

Over the summer of 1903, each side tried to gather up all the evidence that would prove its version of the border was correct. They searched for old maps, letters and other treaties to send to their teams, who were meeting in London.

The British were especially worried. Canada was still part of the British Empire and they wanted to help, but they thought Canada had a very unconvincing argument. But their bigger problem was that everyone in Europe was afraid a big war was about to start with Germany. So the last thing the British wanted was to make an enemy of the U.S. over some (to them) small pieces of land far away.

The Emperor of Germany, known as Kaiser Wilhelm, thought all of this was a great opportunity to start a fight between Britain and America. He sent spies to Alaska to try to stir up trouble.[4]

President Roosevelt, meanwhile, was sure the U.S. map was right. He said he was going to be "ugly" if things didn't go his way. The U.S. had just captured Cuba and the Philippines in a war with Spain in 1898. President Roosevelt was a war hero from that war. He was ready to fight the British and Canadians too. In fact, he once said that a war with Britain might be a great chance to capture all of Canada.

To make sure the Canadian and British negotiators understood this, President Roosevelt sent 800 U.S. soldiers to Alaska. At the same time a friend of the president's was visiting important politicians in England, so President Roosevelt sent him a "secret" letter saying that if the Tribunal didn't make the "right" decision, he would get the U.S. Army to draw the line whether the Canadians liked it or not.

---

4. Kip, once again, we don't make things up in school essays. No one would believe there were German spies in the Yukon!—Mr. Galpin. (Editor's Note: there was no evidence of German Intelligence being involved in the Alaska-Canada dispute until the recent publication of Kip Dutoit's papers. It is worth noting, however, that German Intelligence attempted in 1917 to dissuade the United States from entering World War One by encouraging Mexico to attack Texas, Arizona and New Mexico. But British codebreakers intercepted a secret German telegram and told the U.S. Government. The subsequent "Zimmerman Telegram" scandal outraged President Wilson and was an important factor in the U.S. joining Britain, France and Canada in that conflict.)

Then he sent another letter to his friend telling him to show the "secret" letter to as many Cabinet Ministers as he could find! "Walk softly and carry a big stick," is how President Roosevelt described it.

Some people say President Roosevelt was bluffing. Others aren't sure.

Anyway, by the summer of 1903 things were really beginning to heat up. That's when Colonel Steele came back to the Yukon to look in the Commissioner's archives, and Captain Richardson of the U.S. Army came to the Yukon to scout the territory in case there was a war.[5] Each side gathered as many papers and old maps as they could find. Each side wrote a small book describing why they were right!

British and Canadian legal experts were worried that Canada's case wasn't very strong. There were even Canadian government maps showing that Skagway was in the United States! But others thought that if you read the original treaty the right way, it said that Skagway should be in Canada.

In September, the six members of the Alaska Boundary Tribunal met in London. They argued for about a month. Some points went Canada's way. Others went to the United States. The three American members were trying hard to get the British member, Lord Alverstone, on their side. So were the Canadians. Lord Alverstone was in a tough position since he wanted to help Canada, but didn't think the treaty really said Skagway should be in Canada. To make things even tougher for him, the British government kept telling him that he

---

5.   Editor's Note: Interestingly, despite the fact that Kip's story describes the secret visits of Colonel Steele and Captain Richardson, neither can be confirmed by other historical documents in official British, American or Canadian archives. The Canadian government was nervous at the time about the future of the Yukon, especially since the International Herald Tribune ran a story in November, 1901 referring to a conspiracy by American miners in the Yukon to "overthrow the local government" and "establish a republic with Dawson City as its capital."

shouldn't do anything that would make President Roosevelt start a war.

The critical moment came in October. They had to make a final decision about Skagway. The two Canadians voted that it was in Canada. But the three Americans voted that it was in the United States. Everyone looked at Lord Alverstone. Finally, he voted with the Americans.

When the final decision was made, there was a huge controversy in Canada. Everyone said that Lord Alverstone had "sold Canada out." The Prime Minister said that Canada had to have more control over its own treaties instead of the British.

But I don't know if Canada would have done any better by itself. Like it or not, President Roosevelt thought he was right and was willing to send in the U.S. Army.

In the end, the border stayed pretty close to where Colonel Steele put it in 1898. And most importantly, there was no war.

> *Kip,*
> *A+! Excellent essay. It's as if you were actually involved! I'm glad to see you finally applying yourself at school. There's more to life than hockey.*
> *Mr. Galpin*
>
> *PS: Nice goal in hockey last night, though! Those Dawson people get so superior if they beat Whitehorse.*

About This Book

This book is fiction, set among true historical events and characters. For example, Sam Steele, Theodore Roosevelt, Dr. Nicholson and Captain Wilds Richardson of the U.S. Army are all real people. The historical events surrounding the disputed Alaska-Canada border crisis did occur in 1903 as described.

But Kip and his part in the story are invented, as are the von Neidlings, Thurston Vanderbilt III, the Liebherrs and the Star Mine. Percy Brown the Piccadilly Dude and Black Moran are Robert Service's creations. The newspaper clippings in each chapter are invented, but illustrate the correct timing of events during the crisis. The three clippings in the epilogue are actual examples of newspaper articles published shortly after the final Tribunal decision.

The historical events and characters are portrayed as accurately as possible, based on what we know today. Where it has been necessary to make minor changes to accommodate the story line, these have been noted in Editor's Notes. In the story, for example, Sam Steele returns to the Yukon in 1903 to search for important diplomatic documents for the delegation in London. In real life, he stayed on duty in South Africa where his frontier experience was a major asset for the South African Constabulary. Nor did Theodore Roosevelt visit Alaska. The Editor's Notes on those pages comment on the discrepencies. All of the photos are real, with the exception of the telegram images and Kip's drawings.

Kip's character is based loosely on the pioneer Yukon boyhood stories of the author's grandfather, Bill Taylor, to whom the book is dedicated. He grew up in Whitehorse early in the 20th Century and went on to play a leading role in Taylor & Drury's, the pioneer Yukon merchants. Bill's father appears in the story as Mr. Taylor. Many of the early Whitehorse photos are from Bill's collection, although most were taken 10–15 years after Kip's story. Other parts of the story and Aurore's character are based on the real-life story of the author's grandmother Aline Arbour Cyr, later Aline Taylor.

She was a young girl in Montreal when her father died in 1917. She, her mother Marie-Ange and little brother Wilbrod moved to the Yukon to join their uncle at Kirkman Creek. The uncle had sent many letters describing Kirkman Creek as a thriving community of which he was a leading (and rich) member. They took the train from Montreal to Vancouver, a ship to Skagway, the train to Whitehorse and went by river to Kirkman Creek. The log cabin, dirt floor and empty larder they found in Kirkman Creek were a shock after living in Montreal. They decided to leave the Yukon. After struggling with English speaking ticket agents as portrayed in *Aurore of the Yukon*, they finally got tickets on the S.S. Princess Sophia from Skagway.

Just before departure, however, Aline's mother fell ill and they missed what turned out to be the S.S. Princess Sophia's last voyage. The ship sank off Vanderbilt Reef with all passengers on its way to Vancouver a few days later.

They ended up staying in Whitehorse, where Aline's mother married Antoine (Tony) Cyr, another francophone Yukon pioneer.

Aline and Bill went to Mr. Galpin's class at Lambert Street School. After they were married, they built the log house still seen at Fifth and Main Street in Whitehorse and raised their family. Their great-grandchildren, Kieran, Aline and Pascale Halliday, illustrated this book.

About the Author

Keith Halliday is passionate about Yukon history. He was born in the Yukon and raised on stories of the pioneer days. He is a descendent of the Taylors and Drurys, Gold Rush era merchants and fur traders. His great-grandmother was Marie-Ange Cyr, who moved in 1917 from Montreal to the Yukon frontier with her children Aline and Wilbrod after her husband died. The story of Marie-Ange, Aline and Wilbrod was the inspiration for the *Aurore of the Yukon* series.

After detours in the diplomatic service in Brussels, study in London and management consulting in Toronto, Keith and his wife Stacy live with their four children in the Yukon, where they intend to stay.

About the Illustrators

Kieran, Aline and Pascale Halliday are fifth generation Yukoners. They live with their parents in Whitehorse, not far from the Telegraph Office, White Pass Train Station and the other locations in this book.

They are already working on the pictures for the next adventures of Aurore, Kip, Papillon and Yves.

About the MacBride Museum

MacBride Museum is the Yukon's first museum. It is a fun, interactive and educational museum that illustrates the overall history of the Yukon. Located on Whitehorse's scenic waterfront at the corner of 1st Avenue and Wood Street, MacBride is open year round. Our galleries explore Yukon Facts and Myths, The Natural World of animals and minerals, a hands-on Discovery Zone for kids, Yukon First Nations plus transportation and mining history. The long-awaited MacBride expansion, opened in the summer of 2007, outlines the Yukon's modern history from early exploration in the 1800's until Whitehorse became the capital of the Yukon in 1953.

Go to *www.macbridemuseum.com* to find out more about MacBride's programs, events, online collection and activities, including MacBride Museum summer camps based on Kip's adventures.

978-0-595-44272-0
0-595-44272-2

LaVergne, TN USA
07 April 2010
178508LV00001B/26/A